Books by V. S. PRITCHETT

When My Girl Comes Home

(1961)

The Sailor, Sense of Humour, and Other Stories

(1956)

The Spanish Temper

(1954)

THESE ARE BORZOI BOOKS,
PUBLISHED IN NEW YORK BY ALFRED·A·KNOPF

When
My Girl Comes Home

When

My Girl Comes Home

by V. S. PRITCHETT

NEW YORK

Alfred · A · Knopf

1961

OF THE STORIES in this volume, the following appeared
originally in *The New Yorker:* "The Wheelbarrow,"
"The Fall," "Just a Little More," "The Necklace," "Citizen," and "The Key to My Heart." "On the Scent" appeared originally in *Gentlemen's Quarterly,* and "The
Snag" in *Encounter* in England. "When My Girl Comes
Home" has not been published previously.

823
P961w
93210

L. C. catalog card number: 61–11482

THIS IS A BORZOI BOOK,
PUBLISHED BY ALFRED A. KNOPF, INC.

FIRST AMERICAN EDITION

T O

My Wife

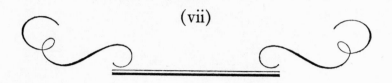

ACKNOWLEDGMENTS

THE AUTHOR presents his acknowledgments to the editors of *The New Yorker, The London Magazine, Encounter, Argosy, The Gentleman's Quarterly,* and *The Compleat Imbiber,* in which all but one of these stories originally appeared

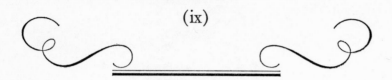

CONTENTS

When
My Girl Comes Home

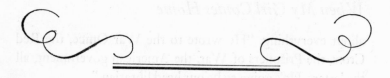

When My Girl Comes Home

She was kissing them all, hugging them, her arms bare in her summer dress, laughing and taking in a big draught of breath after every kiss, nearly knocking old Mrs. Draper off her feet, almost wrestling with Mrs. Fulmino, who was large and tall. Then Hilda broke off to give another foreign-sounding laugh and plunged at Jack Draper ("the baby") and his wife, at Mr. Fulmino, who cried out: "What, again?" and at Constance, who did not like emotion; and after every kiss, Hilda drew back, getting her breath and making this sound like "Hah!"

"Who is this?" she said, looking at me.

"Harry Fraser," Mr. Fulmino said. "You remember Harry?"

"You worked at the grocer's," she said. "I remember you."

"No," I said, "that was my brother."

"This is the little one," said Mrs. Fulmino.

"Who won the scholarship," said Constance.

"We couldn't have done anything without him," said Mr. Fulmino, expanding with extravagance as he always did

3

about everything. "He wrote to the War Office, the Red Cross, the Prisoners of War, the American government, all the letters. He's going to be our head librarian."

Mr. Fulmino loved whatever had not happened yet. His forecasts were always wrong. I left the library years ago and never fulfilled the future he had planned for me. Obviously Hilda did not remember me. Thirteen years before, when she married Mr. Singh and left home, I was no more than a boy.

"Well, I'll kiss him too," she said. "And another for your brother."

That was the first bad thing to happen, the first of many signs of how her life had had no contact with ourselves.

"He was killed in the war, dear," said Mrs. Fulmino.

"She couldn't know," said Constance.

"I'm sorry," said Hilda.

We all stood silent, and Hilda turned to hold on to her mother, little Mrs. Johnson, whose face was coquettish with tears and who came up only to Hilda's shoulder. The old lady was bewildered. She was trembling as though she were going to shake to pieces like a tree in the autumn. Hilda stood still, touching her tinted brown hair, which was done in a tight, high style and still unloosened, despite all the hugs and kissings. Her arms looked as dry as sand, her breasts were full in her green, flowered dress, and she was gazing over our heads now from large yellow eyes that had almost closed into two blind, blissful curving lines. Her eyebrows seemed to be lacquered. How Oriental she looked on that first day! She was looking above our heads at old Mrs. Draper's shabby room and going over the odd things she remembered, and while she stood like that, the women

4

were studying her clothes. A boy's memory is all wrong. Naturally, when I was a boy I had thought of her as tall. She was really short. But I did remember her bold nose: it was like her mother's and old Mrs. Draper's; those two were sisters. Otherwise I wouldn't have known her. And that is what Mr. Fulmino said when we were all silent and incredulous again. We had Hilda back. Not just "back," either, but "back from the dead," reborn.

"She was in the last coach of the train, wasn't she, Mother?" Mr. Fulmino said to Mrs. Johnson. He called her "Mother" for the occasion, celebrating her joy.

"Yes," said Mrs. Johnson. "Yes." Her voice scraped and trembled.

"In the last coach, next the van. We went right up the platform, we thought we'd missed her, didn't we? She was," he exclaimed with acquisitive pride, "in the first class."

"Like you missed me coming from Penzance," said Mrs. Fulmino, swelling powerfully and going that thundery violet colour which old wrongs gave her.

"Posh!" said Hilda. And we all smiled in a sickly way.

"Don't you ever do it again, my girl! Don't you ever do it again," said her mother, old Mrs. Johnson, clinging to her daughter's arm and shaking it as if it were a bell rope.

"I was keeping an eye on my luggage," Hilda said, laughing.

Ah! That was a point! There was not only Hilda, there was her luggage. Some of it was in the room, but the bigger things were outside on the landing, piled up, looking very new, with the fantastic labels of hotels in Tokyo, San Francisco, and New York on it, and a beautiful jewel box in white leather on top like a crown. Old Mrs. Draper did

5

not like the luggage being outside the room in case it was in the way of the people upstairs. Constance went out and fetched the jewel box in. We had all seen it. We were as astonished by all these cases as we were by Hilda herself. After thirteen years, six of them war, we recognized that the poor ruined woman we had prepared for had not arrived. She shone with money. Later on, one after the other of us, except old Mrs. Draper, who could not walk far, went out and looked at the luggage and came back to study Hilda in a new way.

We had all had a shock. She had been nearly two years coming home from Tokyo. Before that there was the occupation; before that the war itself. Before that there were the years in Bombay and Singapore, when she was married to an Indian they always called Mr. Singh. All those years were lost to us. None of us had been to India. What happened there to Mr. Singh? We knew he had died—but how? Even if we had known, we couldn't have imagined it. None of us had been to Singapore, none of us to Japan. People from streets like Hincham Street do go to such places: it is not past belief. Knock on the doors of half the houses in London and you will find people with relations all over the world. But none of us had. Mention these places to us, we look at our grey skies and see boiling sun. Our one certainty about Hilda was what, in fact, the newspaper said the next day, with her photograph and the headline: A MOTHER'S FAITH. FOUR YEARS IN JAPANESE TORTURE CAMP. LONDON GIRL'S ORDEAL. Hilda was a terrible item of news, a gash in our lives, and we looked for the signs of it on her body, in the way she stood, in the lines on her face, as if we were expecting a scream from her mouth like the screams we

6

were told Bill Williams gave out at night in his sleep, after
he had been flown back home when the war ended. We had
had to wait and wait for Hilda. At one time—there was a
postcard from Hawaii—she was pinned like a butterfly in
the middle of the Pacific Ocean; soon after there was a letter from Tokyo saying she couldn't get a passage. Confus-
ing. She was travelling backwards. Letters from Tokyo
were still coming after her letters from San Francisco.

We were still standing, waiting for Constance to bring
in the teapot, for the tea was already laid. The trolley buses
go down Hincham Street. It is a mere one hundred and
fifty yards of a few little houses and a few little shops,
which has a sudden charmed importance because the main
road has petered out at our end by the Lord Nelson and an
enormous public lavatory, and the trolley buses have to run
down Hincham Street before picking up the main road
again, after a sharp turn at the convent. Hincham Street is
less a street than an interval, a disheartened connexion.
While we stood in one of those silences that follow excitement, a trolley bus came by and Hilda exclaimed:

"You've still got the old trams. Bump! Bump! Bump!"
Hilda was ecstatic about the sound. "Do you remember I
used to be frightened the spark from the pole would set the
lace curtains on fire when I was little?"

For as the buses turned, the trolley arms would come
swooping with two or three loud bumps and a spit of blue
electricity, almost hitting Mrs. Draper's sitting-room window, which was on the first floor.

"It's trolleys now, my girl," said old Mrs. Draper, whose
voice was like the voice of time itself chewing away at life.
"The trams went years ago, before the war."

7

Old Mrs. Draper had sat down in her chair again by the fire that always burned winter and summer in this room; she could not stand for long. It was the first remark that had given us any sense of what was bewildering all of us: the passing of time, the growing of a soft girl into a grown, hard-hipped woman. For old Mrs. Draper's mind was detached from events around her and moved only among the signal facts and conclusions of history.

Presently we were, as the saying is, "at our teas." Mr. Fulmino, less puzzled than the rest of us, expanded in his chair with the contentment of one who had personally operated a deeply British miracle. It was he who had got Hilda home.

"We've got all the correspondence, haven't we, Harry?" he said. "We kept it—the War Office, Red Cross, Prisoner of War Commission—everything, Hilda. I'll show it to you."

His task had transformed him and his language. Identification, registration, accommodation, communication, rehabilitation, hospitalization, administration, investigation, transportation—well, we had all dreamed of Hilda in our different ways.

"They always said the same thing," Mrs. Fulmino said reproachfully. "No one of the name of Mrs. Singh on the lists."

"I wrote to Bombay," said Mr. Fulmino.

"He wrote to Singapore," said Mrs. Fulmino.

Mr. Fulmino drank some tea, wiped his lips, and became geography. "All British subjects were rounded up, they said," Mrs. Fulmino said.

8

We nodded. We had made our stand, of course, on the law. Mrs. Fulmino was authority.

"But Hilda was married to an Indian," said Constance.

We glanced with a tolerance we did not usually feel for Constance. She was always trying to drag politics in.

"She's a British subject by birth," said Mrs. Fulmino firmly.

"Mum," Hilda whispered, squeezing her mother's arm hard, and then looked up to listen, as if she were listening to talk about a faraway stranger. "I was in Tokyo when the war started," she said. "Not Singapore."

"Oh, Tokyo," exclaimed Mr. Fulmino, feeling in his waistcoat for a pencil to make a note of it and, suddenly, realizing that his note-taking days were over.

"Whatever the girl has done she has been punished for it," came old Mrs. Draper's mournful voice from the chair by the fire; but in the clatter no one heard her, except old Mrs. Johnson, who squeezed her daughter's arm and said:

"My girl is a jewel."

Still, Hilda's words surprised us. We had worked it out that after she and Mr. Singh were married and went to Bombay, he had heard of a better job in the state railway medical service and had gone to Singapore, where the war had caught her. Mrs. Fulmino looked affronted. If Mr. Fulmino expanded into geography and the language of state—he worked for the Borough Council—Mrs. Fulmino liked a fact to be a fact.

"We got the postcards," said Mrs. Fulmino, sticking to chronology.

"Hawaii," Mr. Fulmino said. "How'd you get there?

9

Swim, I suppose." He added: "A sweet spot, it looks. Suit us for a holiday—palms."

"Coconuts," said young Jack Draper, who worked in a pipe factory, speaking for the first time.

"Be quiet," said his wife.

"It's an American base now," said Constance with her politically sugared smile.

We hesitated but let her observation pass. It was simple to ignore her. We were happy.

"I suppose they paid your fare," said Jack Draper's wife, a north-country woman.

"Accommodation, transportation," said Mr. Fulmino, "food, clothing. Everything. Financed by the international commission."

This remark made old Mrs. Johnson cry a little. In those years none of us had deeply believed that Hilda was alive. The silence was too long; too much time had gone by. Others had come home by the thousand with stories of thousands who had died. Only old Mrs. Johnson had been convinced that Hilda was safe. The landlord at the Lord Nelson, the butcher, anyone who met old Mrs. Johnson as she walked by like a poor, decent ghost with her sewing bundles, in those last two years, all said in war-staled voices:

"It's a mother's faith, that's what it is. A mother's faith's a funny thing."

She would walk along with a cough, like someone driving tacks. Her chest had sunk and under her brown coat her shoulder blades seemed to have sharpened into a single hump. Her faith gave her a bright, yet also a sly, dishonest look.

"I'm taking this sewing up to Mrs. Tracy's. She wants it in a hurry," she might say.

"You ought to rest, Mrs. Johnson, like the doctor said."

"I want a bit of money for when my girl comes home," she said. "She'll want feeding up."

And she would look around, perhaps, for a clock, in case she ought, by this time, to have put a pot on the stove.

She had been too ill, in hospital, during the war, to speak about what might have happened to Hilda. Her own pain and fear of dying deafened her to what could be guessed. Mrs. Johnson's faith had been born out of pain, out of the inability—within her prison of aching bones and crushed breathing—to identify herself with her daughter. Her faith grew out of her very self-centredness. And when she came out from the post office every week, where she put her savings, she looked demure, holy, and secretive. If people were too kind and too sympathetic with her, she shuffled and looked mockingly. Seven hospitals, she said, had not killed *her*.

Now, when she heard Mr. Fulmino's words about the fare, the clothes, the food, the expense of it all, she was troubled. What had she worked for—even at one time scrubbing in a canteen—but to save Hilda from a charity so vast in its humiliation, from so blank a herding mercy. Hilda was hers, not theirs. Hilda kept her arm on her mother's waist, and while Mr. Fulmino carried on with the marvels of international organization (which moved Mrs. Fulmino to say hungrily: "It takes a war to bring it out"), Hilda ignored them and whispered to comfort her mother. At last the old lady dried her eyes and smiled at her daughter. The smile grew to a small laugh, she gave a proud jerk to her head, conveying that she and her Hil were not going to kowtow in gratitude to anyone, and Hilda, at last, said out loud to her mother what, no doubt, she had been whispering.

"He wouldn't let me pay anything, Mum. Faulkner, his name was. Very highly educated. He came from California. We had a fancy-dress dance on the ship and he made me go as a geisha. . . . He gave me these. . . ." And she raised her hand to show her mother the bracelets on it.

Mrs. Johnson laughed wickedly. "Did he . . . ? Was he . . . ?" said Mrs. Johnson.

"No. Well, I don't know," said Hilda. "But I kept his address."

Mrs. Johnson smiled round at all of us, to show that in spite of all, being the poorest in the family and the ones that had suffered most, she and Hilda knew how to look after themselves.

This was the moment when there was that knock on the door. Everyone was startled and looked at it.

"A knock!" said Mr. Fulmino.

"A knock, Constance," said young Mrs. Draper, who had busy north-country ears.

"A knock," several said.

Old Mrs. Draper made one of her fundamental utterances again, one of her growls from the belly of the history of human indignation.

"We are," she said, "in the middle of our teas. Constance, go and see and tell them."

But before Constance got to the door, two young men, one with a camera, came right into the room, without asking. Some of us lowered our heads and then, just as one young man said "I'm from the *News*," the other clicked his camera.

Jack Draper said, nearly choking: "He's taken a snap of us eating."

While we were all staring at them, old Mrs. Draper chewed out grandly: "Who may they be?"

But Hilda stood up and got her mother to her feet, too. "Stand up all of us," she said eagerly. "It's for the papers."

It was the Press. We were in confusion. Mrs. Fulmino pushed Mr. Fulmino forward towards the reporter and then pulled him back. The reporter stood asking questions and everyone answered at once. The photographer kept on taking photographs and, when he was not doing that, started picking up vases and putting them down and one moment was trying the drawer of a little table by the window. They pushed Hilda and her mother into a corner and took a picture of them, Hilda calling to us all to "come in" and Mr. Fulmino explaining to the reporters. Then they went, leaving a cigarette burning on one of old Mrs. Draper's lace doilies under the fern and two more butts on the floor. "What did they say? What did they say?" we all asked one another, but no one could remember. We were all talking at once, arguing about who had heard the knock first. Young Mrs. Draper said her tea was spoiled, and Constance opened the window to let the cigarette smoke out and then got the kettle. Mr. Fulmino put his hand on his wife's knee because she was upset, and she shook it off. When we had calmed down, Hilda said:

"The young one was a nice-looking boy, wasn't he, Mum?" and Mr. Fulmino, who almost never voiced the common opinion about anything but who had perhaps noticed how the eyes of all the women went larger at this remark, laughed loudly and said:

"We've got the old Hilda back!"

I mention this because of the item in the papers next day: A MOTHER'S FAITH. FOUR YEARS IN JAPANESE TORTURE CAMP. LONDON GIRL'S ORDEAL.

Wonderful, as Mr. Fulmino said.

To be truthful, I felt uncomfortable at old Mrs. Draper's. They were not my family. I had been dragged there by Mr. Fulmino, and by a look now and then from young Mrs. Draper and from Constance, I had the feeling that they thought it was indecent for me to be there when I had only been going with Iris, Mr. Fulmino's daughter, for two or three months. I had to be tolerated as one more example of Mr. Fulmino's uncontrollable gift—the gift for colonizing.

Mr. Fulmino had shot up from nothing during the war. It had given him personality. He was a short, talkative, heavy man of forty-five with a wet gold tooth and glossy black hair that streamlined back across his head from an arrow point, getting thin in front. His eyes were anxious, overworked, and puddled; indeed, if you had not known him you would have thought he had had a couple of black eyes that had never got right. He bowled along as he walked, like someone absorbed by fondness for his own body. He had been in many things before he got to work for the Council—the army (but not a fighting soldier) in the war, in auctions, and at the bar of a club. He was very active, confiding and enquiring.

When I first met him I was working at the counter of the

public library, during the war, and one day he came over from the Council officers and said, importantly:

"Friend, we've got a bit of a headache. We've got an enquiry from the War Office. Have you got anything about Malaya—with maps?"

In the next breath he was deflating himself.

"It's a personal thing. They never tell you anything. I've got a niece out there."

Honesty made him sound underhand. His manner suggested that his niece was a secret fortification somewhere east of Suez. Soon he was showing me the questionnaire from the Red Cross. Then he was telling me that his wife, like the rest of the Drapers, was very handsome—"A lovely woman" in more ways, his manner suggested, than one— but that since Hilda had gone, she had become a different woman. The transition from handsome to different was, he suggested, a catastrophe that he was obliged to share with the public. He would come in from fire-watching, he said, and find her demented. In bed, he would add. He and I found ourselves fire-watching together, and from that time he started facetiously calling me "my secretary."

"I asked my secretary to get the sand and shovel out," he would say about our correspondence, "and he wrote the letter."

So I was half a stranger at Hilda's homecoming. I looked round the room or out at the shops opposite, and when I looked back at the family several times I caught Hilda's eyes wandering too. She also was out of it. I studied her. I hadn't expected her to come back in rags, as old Mrs. Draper had, but it was a surprise to see she was the best-dressed woman in the room and the only one who looked

as if she had ever been to a hairdresser. And there was another way in which I could not match her with the person
Mr. Fulmino and I had conjured up. When we thought of
everything that must have happened to her, it was strange
to see that her strong face was smooth and blank. Except for
the few minutes of arrival and the time the reporters came,
her face was vacant and plain. It was as vacant as a stone
that had been smoothed for centuries in the sand of some hot
country. It was the face of someone to whom nothing had
happened; or, perhaps, so much had happened to her that
each event wiped out what had happened before. I was disturbed by something in her—the lack of history, I think.
We were worm-eaten by it. And that suddenly brought her
back to me as she had been when she was a schoolgirl and
when my older brother got into trouble for chasing after
her. She was now sharper in the shoulders and elbows, no
longer the swollen schoolgirl, but, even as a girl, her face
had had the same quality of having been fixed and un-
changeable between its high cheekbones. It was disturbing,
in a face so anonymous, to see the eyes move, especially
since she blinked very little; and if she smiled it was less a
smile than an alteration of the two lines at the corners of
her lips.

The party did not settle down quite in the same way
after the reporters had been, and there was talk of not tiring
Hilda after her long journey. The family would all be meeting tomorrow, the Sunday, as they always did, when young
Mrs. Jack Draper brought her children. Jack Draper was
thinking of the pub, which was open now, and asking if
anyone was going over. And then, something happened.

16

Hilda walked over to the window to Mr. Fulmino and said, just as if she had not been there at the time:

"Ted, what did that man from the *News* ask you—about the food?"

"No," said Mr. Fulmino, widening to a splendid chance of not giving the facts. "No—he said something about starving the prisoners. I was telling him that in my opinion the deterioration in conditions was inevitable after the disorganization in the camps resulting from air operations. . . ."

"Oh, I thought you said we starved. We had enough."

"What?" said Mr. Fulmino.

"Bill Williams was a skeleton when he came back. Nothing but a bowl of rice a day. Rice!" said Mrs. Fulmino. "And torture."

"Bill Williams must have been in one of those labour camps," said Hilda. "Being Japanese, I was all right."

"Japanese!" said Mr. Fulmino. "You?"

"Shinji was a Japanese," said Hilda. "He was in the army."

"You married a Japanese!" said Mrs. Fulmino, marching forward.

"That's why I was put in the American camp, when they came. They questioned every one, not only me. That's what I said to the reporter. It wasn't the food, it was the questions. What was his regiment? When did you hear from him? What was his number? They kept on. Didn't they, Mum?"

She turned to her mother, who had taken the chance to cut herself another piece of cake and was about to slip it into her handkerchief, I think, to carry to her own room.

We were all flabbergasted. A trolley bus went by and took a swipe at the wall. Young Mrs. Draper murmured something, and her young husband, Jack, hearing his wife, said loudly:

"Hilda married a Nip!"

And he looked at Hilda with astonishment. He had very blue eyes.

"You weren't a prisoner!" said Mrs. Fulmino.

"Not of the Japanese," said Hilda. "They couldn't touch me. My husband was Japanese.

"I'm not stupid. I can hear," said young Mrs. Draper to her husband. She was a plain-spoken woman from the Yorkshire coal fields, one of a family of twelve.

"I've nowt to say about who you married, but where is he? Haven't you brought him?" she said.

"You were married to Mr. Singh," said Mrs. Fulmino.

"They're both dead," said Hilda, her vacant yellow eyes becoming suddenly brilliant like a cat's at night. An animal sound, like the noise of an old dog at a bone, came out of old Mrs. Draper by the fire.

"Two," she moaned.

No more than that. Simply, again: "Two."

Hilda was holding her handbag and she lifted it in both hands and covered her bosom with it. Perhaps she thought we were going to hit her. Perhaps she was going to open the bag and get out something extraordinary—documents, letters, or a handkerchief to weep into. But no—she held it there very tight. It was an American handbag; we hadn't seen one like that before, cream-coloured, like the luggage. Old Mrs. Johnson hesitated at the table, tipped the piece of cake back out of her handkerchief onto a plate, and stepped to Hilda's side and stood, very straight for once, beside her, the old blue lips very still.

"Ted," accused Hilda. "Didn't you get my letters? Mother"—she stepped away from her mother—"didn't you tell them?"

"What, dear?" said old Mrs. Johnson.

"About Shinji. I wrote you. Did Mum tell you?" Hilda appealed to us and now looked fiercely at her mother.

Mrs. Johnson smiled and retired into her look of faith and modesty. She feigned deafness.

"I put it all in the post office," she said. "Every week," she said. " 'Until my girl comes home,' I said. 'She'll need it.' "

"Mother!" said Hilda, giving the old lady a small shake. "I wrote to you. I told you. Didn't you tell them?"

"What did Hilda say?" said Mr. Fulmino gently, bending down to the old lady.

"Sh! Don't worry her. She's had enough for today. What did you tell the papers, Ted?" said Mrs. Fulmino, turning on her husband. "You can't ever keep your big mouth shut, can you? You never let me see the correspondence."

"I married Shinji when the war came up," Hilda said.

And then old Mrs. Draper spoke from her armchair by the fire. She had her bad leg propped up on a hassock.

"Two," said Mrs. Draper savagely again.

Mr. Fulmino, in his defeat, lost his nerve and let slip a remark quite casually, as he thought, under his voice, but everyone heard it—a remark that Mrs. Fulmino was to remind him of in months to come.

"She strikes like a clock," he said.

We were stupefied by Mr. Fulmino's remark. Perhaps it was a relief.

"Mr. Fraser!" Hilda said to me. And now her vacant face had become dramatic and she stepped towards me, appealing outside the family. "You knew, you and Ted knew. You've got all the letters. . . ."

If ever a man looked like the captain going down with his ship and suddenly conscious, at the last heroic moment, that he is not on a ship at all, but standing on nothing and had hopelessly blundered, it was Mr. Fulmino. But we didn't go down, either of us. For suddenly old Mrs. Johnson couldn't stand straight any longer; her head wagged and drooped forward, and but for a chair, she would have fallen to the ground.

"Quick! Constance! Open the window," Mrs. Fulmino said. Hilda was on her knees by her mother.

"Are you there, Hilly?" said her mother.

"Yes, I'm here, Mum," said Hilda. "Get some water— some brandy." They took the old lady next door to the little room Hilda was sharing with her that night.

"What I can't fathom is your aunt not telling me, keeping it to herself," said Mr. Fulmino to his wife as we walked home that evening from Mrs. Draper's, and we had said goodbye to Jack Draper and his wife.

He was not hurt by Mrs. Johnson's secretiveness but by an extraordinary failure of co-operation.

It was unwise of him to criticize Mrs. Fulmino's family.

"Don't be so smug," said Mrs. Fulmino. "What's it got to do with you? She was keeping it from Gran: you know

Gran's tongue. She's her sister." They called old Mrs. Draper "Gran" or "Grandma" sometimes.

But when Mr. Fulmino got home he asked me in so that we could search the correspondence together. Almost at once we discovered his blunder. There it was in the letter saying a Mrs. Singh or Shinji Kobayashi had been identified.

"Shinji!" exclaimed Mrs. Fulmino, putting her big index finger on the page. "There you are, plain as dirt."

"Singh," said Mr. Fulmino. "Singh, Shinji, the same name. Some Indians write Singh, some Shinji."

"And what is Kobayashi? Indian too? Don't be a fool."

"It's the family name or Christian name of Singh," said Mr. Fulmino, doing the best he could.

"Singh, Shinji, Shinji, Singh," he murmured to himself, and he walked about trying to convince himself by incantation and hypnosis. He lashed himself with Kobayashi. He remembered the names of other Indians, Indian cities, mentioned the Ganges and the Himalayas; had a brief, brilliant couple of minutes when he argued that Shinji was Hindu for Singh. Mrs. Fulmino watched him with the detachment of one waiting for a bluebottle to settle so that she could swat it.

"*You* thought Kobayashi was Indian, didn't you, Harry?" he appealed to me. I did my best.

"I thought," I said weakly, "it was the address."

"Ah, the address!" Mr. Fulmino clutched at this, but he knew he was done for. Mrs. Fulmino struck.

"And what about the Sunday papers, the man from the *News?*" she said. "You open your big mouth too soon."

. . .

When My Girl Comes Home

"Christ!" said Mr. Fulmino. It was the sound of a man who has gone to the floor.

I will come to that matter of the papers later on. It is not very important.

When we went to bed that night we must all have known in our different ways that we had been disturbed in a very long dream. We had been living on inner visions for years. It was an effect of the long war. England had been a prison. Even the sky was closed, and, like convicts, we had been driven to dwelling on fancies in our dreary minds. In the cinema the camera sucks some person forward into an enormous close-up and holds a face there yards wide, filling the whole screen, all holes and pores, like some sucking octopus that might eat up an audience many rows at a time. I don't say these pictures aren't beautiful sometimes, but afterwards I get the horrors. Hilda had been a close-up like this for us when she was lost and far away. For myself, I could hardly remember Hilda. She was a collection of fragments of my childhood and I suppose I had expected a girl to return.

My father and mother looked down on the Drapers and the Johnsons. Hincham Street was "dirty," and my mother once whispered that Mr. Johnson had worked "on the line," as if that were a smell. I remember the old man's huge, crinkled, white beard when I was a child. It was horribly soft and like pubic hair. So I had always thought of Hilda as a railway girl, in and out of tunnels, signal boxes, and main-line stations, and when my older brother was "chasing" her as they said, I admired him. I listened to the quarrels that went on in our family: how she had gone to the convent school and the nuns had complained about her; and was it she or some other girl who went for car rides with a married man who waited round the corner of Hincham Street for her? The sinister phrase "The nuns have been to see her mother" stuck in my memory. It astonished me to see Hilda alive, calm, fat, and walking after that, as composed as a railway engine. When I grew up and Mr. Fulmino came to the library, I was drawn into his search because she brought back those days with my brother, those clouts on the head from some friend of his, saying: "Buzz off. Little pigs have big ears," when my brother and he were whispering about her.

To Mrs. Fulmino, a woman whose feelings were in her rolling arms, flying out from one extreme to another as she talked, as if she were doing exercises, Hilda appeared in her wedding clothes and all the sexuality of an open flower, standing beside her young Indian husband, who was about to become a doctor. There was trouble about the wedding, for Mr. Singh spoke a glittering and palatial English—the beautiful English a snake might speak, it seemed to the family—that made a few pock marks on his face somehow more noticeable. Old Mrs. Draper alone, against all evidence —Mr. Singh had had a red racing car—stuck to it that he was "a common Lascar off a ship." Mrs. Fulmino had been terrified of Mr. Singh, she often conveyed, and had "refused to be in a room alone with him." Or "How can she let him touch her?" she would murmur, thinking about that, above all. Then whatever vision was in her mind would jump forward to Hilda captured, raped, tortured, murdered in front of her eyes. Mrs. Fulmino's mind was voluptuous.

When I first went to Mr. Fulmino's house and met Iris and we talked about Hilda, Mrs. Fulmino once or twice left the room and he lowered his voice. "The wife's upset," he said. "She's easily upset."

We had not all been under a spell. Not young Jack Draper or his wife, for example. Jack Draper had fought in the war, and whereas we thought of the war as something done to us and our side, Jack thought of it as something done to everybody. I remember what he said to his wife before the Fulminos and I said good night to them on the Saturday Hilda came home.

"It's a shame," said Jack, "she couldn't bring the Nip with her."

"He was killed," said his wife.

"That's what I mean," said Jack. "It's a bleeding shame she couldn't."

We walked on and then young Mrs. Draper said, in her flat, northern, laconic voice:

"Well, Jack, for all the to-do, you might just as well have gone to your fishing."

For Jack had made a sacrifice in coming to welcome Hilda. He went fishing up the Thames on Saturdays. The war for him was something that spoiled fishing. In the Normandy landing he had thought mostly of that. He dreamed of the time when his two boys would be old enough to fish. It was what he had had children for.

"There's always Sunday," said his wife, tempting him. Jack nodded. She knew he would not fall. He was the youngest of old Mrs. Draper's family, the baby, as they said. He never missed old Mrs. Draper's Sundays.

. . .

It was a good thing he did not, a good thing for all of us that we didn't miss, for we would have missed Hilda's second announcement.

Young Mrs. Draper provoked it. These Sunday visits to Hincham Street were a ritual in the family. It was a duty to old Mrs. Draper. We went there for our tea. She provided, though Constance prepared for it as if we were a school, for she kept house there. We recognized our obligation by paying sixpence into the green pot on the chiffonier when we left. The custom had started in the bad times when money was short; but now this money was regarded as capital, and Jack Draper used to joke and say: "Who are you going to leave the green pot to, Mum?" Some of Hilda's luggage had been moved by the afternoon into her mother's little room at the back, and how those two could sleep in a bed so small was a question raised by Mrs. Fulmino, whose night with Mr. Fulmino required room for struggle, as I know, for this colonizing man often dropped hints about how she swung her legs over in the night.

"Have you unpacked yet, Hilda?" Mrs. Fulmino was asking.

"Unpacked!" said Constance. "Where would she put all that?"

"I've been lazy," said Hilda. "I've just hung up a few things because of the creases."

"Things do crease," said Mrs. Fulmino.

"Bill Williams said he would drop in later," said Constance.

"That man suffered," said Mrs. Fulmino, with meaning.

"He heard you were back," said Constance.

Hilda had told us about Shinji. Jack Draper listened with

25

wonder. Shinji had been in the jute business, and when the war came he was called up to the army. He was in Stores. Jack scratched with delight when he heard this. "Same as I tried to work it," Jack said. Shinji had been killed in an air raid. Jack's wife said, to change the subject, she liked that idea, the idea of Jack "working" anything; he always let everyone climb up on his shoulders. "First man to get wounded. I knew he would be," she said. "He never looks where he's going."

"Is that the Bill Williams who worked for Ryan, the builder?" said Hilda.

"He lives in the Culverwell Road," young Mrs. Draper said.

Old Mrs. Draper, speaking from the bowels of history, said: "He got that Sellers girl into trouble."

"Yes," exclaimed Hilda, "I remember."

"It was proved in court that he didn't," said Constance briskly to Hilda. "You weren't here."

We were all silent. One could hear only the sounds of our cups on the saucers and Mrs. Fulmino's murmur: "More bread and butter?" Constance's face had its neat, pink, enamelled smile, and one saw the truthful blue of her small eyes become purer in colour. Iris was next to me and she said afterwards something I hadn't noticed, that Constance hated Hilda. It is one of the difficulties I have in writing, that, all along, I was slow to see what was really happening, not having a woman's eye or ear. And being young. Old Mrs. Draper spoke again, her mind moving from the past to the present with that suddenness old people have.

"If Bill Williams is coming, he knows the way," she said.

26

Hilda understood that remark, for she smiled and Constance flushed. (Of course, I see it now: two women in a house! Constance had ruled old Mrs. Draper and Mrs. Johnson for years and her money had made a big difference.) They knew that one could, as the saying is, "trust Gran to put her oar in."

Again, young Mrs. Draper changed the subject. She was a nimble, tarry-haired woman, impatient of fancies, excitements, and disasters. She liked things flat and factual. While the family gaped at Hilda's clothes and luggage, young Mrs. Draper had reckoned up the cost of them. She was not avaricious or mean, but she knew that money is money. You know that if you have done without. So she went straight into the important question, being (as she would say) not like people in the south, double-faced Wesleyans, but honest, plain, and straight out with it, what are they ashamed of? Jack, her husband, was frightened by her bluntness, and had the nervous habit of folding his arms across his chest and scratching fast under his armpits when his wife spoke out about money; some view of the river, with his bait and line and the evening flies, came into his panicking mind. Mr. Fulmino once said that Jack scratched because the happiest moments of his life, the moments of escape, had been passed in clouds of gnats.

"I suppose, Hilda, you'll be thinking of what you're going to do?" young Mrs. Draper said. "Did they give you a pension?"

I was stroking Iris's knee but she stopped me, alerted like the rest of them. The word "pension" is a very powerful word. In this neighbourhood one could divide the world into those who had pensions and those who hadn't. The phrase "the old pensioner" was one of envy, abuse, and admiration. My father, for example, spoke contemptuously of pensioners. Old Mrs. Draper's husband had had a pension, but my father would never have one. As a librarian, Mr. Fulmino pointed out, I would have a pension and thereby I had overcome the first obstacle in being allowed to go out with his daughter.

"No," said Hilda, "nothing."

"But he was your husband, you said," said Constance.

"He was in the army, you say," said young Mrs. Draper.

"Inflation," said Mr. Fulmino grandly. "The financial situation."

He was stopped.

"Then," said young Mrs. Draper, "you'll have to go to work."

"My girl won't want for money," said old Mrs. Johnson, sitting beside her daughter as she had done the day before.

"No," said young Mrs. Draper, "that she won't while you're alive, Mrs. Johnson. We all know that, and the way you slaved for her. But Hilda wants to look after you, I'm sure."

It was, of course, the question in everyone's mind. Did all those clothes and cases mean money or was it all show? That is what we all wanted to know. We would not have raised it at that time and in that way. It wasn't our way; we would have drifted into finding out—Hilda was scarcely home. But young Mrs. Draper had been brought up hard, she said, twelve mouths to feed.

"*I'm* looking after *you*, Mum," said Hilda, smiling at her mother.

Mrs. Johnson was like a wizened little girl gazing up at a taller sister.

"I'll take you to Monte Carlo, Mum," Hilda said.

The old lady tittered. We all laughed loudly. Hilda laughed with us.

"That gambling place!" the old lady giggled.

"That's it," laughed Hilda. "Break the bank."

"Is it across water?" said the old lady, playing up. "I couldn't go on a boat. I was so sick at Southend when I was a girl."

"Then we'll fly."

"Oh!" the old lady screeched. "Don't, Hil—I'll have a fit."

"The man who broke the bank at Monte Carlo," Mr. Fulmino sang. "You might find a boy-friend, Mrs. Johnson."

Young Mrs. Draper did not laugh at this game; she still wanted to know; but she did smile. She was worried by laughter. Constance did not laugh but she showed her pretty white teeth.

"Oh, she's got one for me," said Mrs. Johnson. "So she says."

"Of course I have. Haven't I, Harry?" said Hilda, talking across the table to me.

"Me? What?" I said, completely startled.

"You can't take Harry," said Iris, half frightened. Until then I did not know that Iris was interested in me.

"Did you post the letter?" said Hilda to me.

"What letter?" said Iris to me. "Did she give you a letter?"

Now, there is a thing I ought to have mentioned! I had forgotten all about the letter. When we were leaving the evening before, Hilda had called me quietly to the door and said:

"Please post this for me. Tonight."

"Hilda gave me a letter to post," I said.

"You did post it?" Hilda said.

"Yes," I said.

She looked contentedly round at everyone.

"I wrote to Mr. Gloster, the gentleman I told you about, on the boat. He's in Paris. He's coming over at the end of the week to get a car. He's taking Mother and me to France. Mr. Gloster, Mum, I told you. No, not Mr. Faulkner. That was the other boat. He was in San Francisco."

"Oh," said Mrs. Johnson, a very long "oh," and wriggling like a child listening to a story. She was beginning to look pale, as she had the evening before when she had her turn.

"France!" said Constance in a peremptory voice.

"Who is Mr. Gloster? You never said anything," said Mrs. Fulmino.

"What about the currency regulations?" said Mr. Fulmino.

Young Mrs. Draper said: "France! He must have money."

"Dollars," said Hilda to Mr. Fulmino.

Dollars! There was a word!

"The almighty dollar," said Constance, in the cleansed and uncorrupted voice of one who has mentioned one of the Commandments. Constance had principles; we had the confusion of our passions.

And from sixteen years or more back in time, or perhaps it was from some point in history hundreds of years back and forgotten, old Mrs. Draper said: "And is this Indian married?"

Hilda, to whom no events, I believe, had ever happened, replied: "Mr. Gloster's an American, Gran."

"He wants to marry her," said old Mrs. Johnson proudly.

"If I'll have him!" said Hilda.

"Well, he can't if you won't have him, can he, Hilda?" said Mrs. Fulmino.

"Gloster. G–L–O–S–T–E–R?" asked Mr. Fulmino.

"Is he in a good job?" asked young Mrs. Draper.

Hilda pointed to a brooch on her blouse. "He gave me this," she said.

She spoke in her harsh voice and with a movement of her face which in anyone else one would have called excited, but in her it had a disturbing lack of meaning. It was as if Hilda had been hooked into the air by invisible wires and was then swept out into the air and back to Japan, thousands of miles away again, and while she was on her way, she turned and knocked us flat with the next item.

"He's a writer," she said. "He's going to write a book about me. He's very interested in me. . . ."

Mrs. Johnson nodded.

"He's coming to fetch us, Mum and me, and take us to France to write this book. He's going to write my life."

Her life! Here was a woman who had, on top of everything else, a life.

"Coming *here?*" said Mrs. Fulmino with a grinding look at old Mrs. Draper and then at Constance, trying to catch their eyes and failing; in despair she looked at the shabby room, to see what must be put straight, or needed cleaning or painting. Nothing had been done to it for years, for Constance, teaching at her school all day and very clean in her person, let things go in the house, and young Mrs. Draper said old Mrs. Draper smelt. All the command in Mrs. Fulmino's face collapsed as rapidly, on her own, she looked at the carpets, the lino, the curtains.

"What's he putting in this book?" said young Mrs. Draper cannily.

"Yes," said Jack Draper, backing up his wife.

"What I tell him," Hilda said.

"What she tells him," said old Mrs. Johnson, sparkling. Constance looked thoughtfully at Hilda.

"Is it a biography?" Constance asked coldly. There were times when we respected Constance and forgot to murmur "Go back to Russia" every time she spoke. I knew what a biography was and so did Mr. Fulmino, but no one else did.

"It's going to be made into a film," Hilda replied.

"A film," cried Iris.

Constance gleamed.

"You watch for American propaganda," said Constance. There you are, you see: Constance was back on it!

"Oh, it's about me," said Hilda. "My experiences."

"Very interesting," said Mr. Fulmino, preparing to take over. "A Hollywood production, I expect. Publication first and then they go into production." He spread his legs.

None of us had believed or even understood what we heard, but we looked at Mr. Fulmino with gratitude for making the world steady again.

Jack Draper's eyes filled with tears because a question was working in him but he could not get it out.

"Will you be in this film?" asked Iris.

"I'll wait till he's written it," said Hilda with that lack of interest we had often noticed in her after she had made some dramatic statement.

Mrs. Fulmino breathed out heavily with relief and after that her body seemed to become larger. She touched her hair at the back and straightened her dress, as if preparing to offer herself for the part. She said indeed:

"I used to act at school."

"She's still good at it," said Mr. Fulmino with daring to Jack Draper, who always appreciated Mr. Fulmino, but, seeing the danger of the moment, hugged himself and scratched excitedly under both armpits, laughing.

"You shouldn't have let this Mr. Gloster go," said Constance.

Hilda was startled by this remark and looked lost. Then she shrugged her shoulders and gave a low laugh, as if to herself.

Mr. Fulmino's joke had eased our bewilderment. Hilda had been our dream, but now she was home she changed as fast as dreams change. She was now, as we looked at her, far more remote to us than she had been all the years when she was away. The idea was so far beyond us. It was like some story of a bomb explosion or an elopement or a picture of bathing girls one sees in the newspapers—unreal and, in a way, insulting to being alive in the ordinary daily sense of the word. Or, she was like a picture one sees in an art gallery which makes you feel sad because it is painted.

After tea, when Hilda took her mother to the lavatory, Constance beckoned to Iris and let her peep into the room Hilda was sharing, and young Mrs. Draper, not to be kept out of things, followed. They were back in half a minute.

"Six evening dresses," Iris said to me.

"She said it was Mr. Faulkner who gave her the luggage, not this one who was going to get her into pictures," said Mrs. Fulmino.

"Mr. Gloster, you mean," said Constance.

Young Mrs. Draper was watching the door, listening for Hilda's return.

"Ssh," she said at the sound of footsteps on the stairs, and to look at us—the men on one side of the room and the women on the other, silent, standing at attention, facing each other—we looked like soldiers.

"Oh," said Constance. The steps we had heard were not Hilda's. It was Bill Williams who came in.

"Good afternoon, one and all," he said. The words came from the corner of a mouth that had slipped down at one side. Constance drew herself up; her eyes softened. She had exact, small, round breasts. Looking around, he said to Constance: "Where is she?"

Constance lowered her head when she spoke to him, though she held it up shining, admiring him, when he spoke to us, as if she were displaying him to us.

"She'll be here in a minute," she said. "She's going into films."

"I'll take a seat in the two and fourpennies," said Bill Williams and he sat down at his ease and lit a cigarette.

Bill Williams was a very tall, sick-faced man who stooped his shoulders as if he were used to ducking under doors. His dry black hair, not oiled like Mr. Fulmino's, bushed over his forehead, and he had the shoulders, arms,

34

and hands of a lorry driver. In fact, he drove a light van for a textile firm. His hazel eyes were always watching and wandering, and we used to say he looked as though he was going to snaffle something, but that may simply have been due to the restlessness of a man with a poor stomach. Laziness, cunning, and aches and pains were suggested by him. He was a man taking his time. His eyebrows grew thick and the way one brow was raised, combined with the side slip of his mouth, made him look like some shrewd man about to pick up a faulty rifle, hit the bull's-eye five times running at a fair, and moan afterwards. He glanced a good deal at Constance. He was afraid of his manners before her, we thought, because he was a rough type.

"Put it here," said Constance, bringing him an ash tray. That was what he was waiting for, for he did not look at her again.

Bill Williams brought discomfort with him whenever he came on Sundays and we were always happier when he failed to come. If there was anything private to say, we tried to get it over before he came. How a woman like Constance, a true, clean, settled schoolteacher who even spoke in the clear, practical, and superior manner of someone used to the voice of reason, who kept her nails so beautifully, could have taken up with him baffled us. He was very often at Mrs. Draper's in the week, eating with them, and Constance, who was thirty-five, quarrelled like a girl when she was getting things ready for him. Mrs. Fulmino could not bear the way he ate, with his elbows out and his face close to the plate. The only good thing about the affair was that, for once, Constance was overruled.

"Listen to her," Bill Williams would say with a nod of

his head. "A rank-red Communist. Tell us about Holy Russia, Connie."

"Constance is my name, not Connie," she said.

Their bickering made us die. But we respected Constance even when she was a trial. She had been twice to Russia before the war, and though we argued violently with her, especially Mr. Fulmino, who tried to take over Russia and populate it with explanations, we always boasted that she'd been there, to other people.

"On delegations," Mr. Fulmino would say.

But we could *not* boast that she had taken up with Bill Williams. He had been a hero when he came back from Japan, but he had never kept a job since, he was rough, and his lazy, zigzagging habits in his work made even Constance impatient. He had for her the fascination a teacher feels for a bad pupil. Lately their love affair had been going better because he was working outside London and sometimes he worked at weekends; this added to the sense of something vague and secretive in his life that had attracted Constance. For there was much that was secret in her, or so she liked to hint: it was political. Again, it was the secretiveness of those who like power; she was the schoolmistress who has the threat of inside knowledge locked up in the cupboard. Once Mrs. Fulmino went purple and said to her husband (who told me; he always told me such things) that she believed Constance had lately started sleeping with Bill Williams. That was because Constance had once said to her:

"Bill and I are individuals."

Mrs. Fulmino had a row with Iris after this and stopped me seeing her for a month.

Hilda came back into the room alone. Bill Williams let his mouth slip sideways and spoke a strange word to her, saying jauntily to us: "That's Japanese."

Hilda wasn't surprised. She replied with a whole sentence in Japanese.

"That means—" Bill Williams was beaten, but he passed it off. "Well, I'd best not tell them what it means," he said.

"East meets East," Mr. Fulmino said.

"It means," said Hilda, "you were on the other side of the fence, but now the gate is open."

Bill Williams studied her inch by inch. He scratched his head. "Straight?" he said.

"Yes," she said.

"Stone me, it was bloody closed when we were there," said Bill Williams offensively, but then said: "They fed her well, didn't they, Constance? Sit down." Hilda sat down beside him.

"Connie!" he called. "Seen these? Just the job, eh?" He was nodding at Hilda's stockings. Nylons. "Now," he said to Hilda, looking closely at her. "Where were you? It got a bit rough at the finish, didn't it?"

Jack Draper came close to them to hear, hoping that Hilda would say something about what moved him the most: the enemy. Bill Williams gave him a wink and Hilda saw it. She looked placidly at Bill Williams, considering his face, his neck, his shoulders, and his hands, which were resting on his knees.

"I was okey doke," she said.

Bill Williams dropped his mouth open and waggled the top of his tongue in a back tooth in his knowing manner. To our astonishment Hilda opened her mouth and gave a neat twist to her tongue in her cheek in the same way.

Bill Williams slapped his knee and, to cover his defeat in this little duel, said to all of us: "This little girl's got yellow eyes."

All the colour had gone from Connie's face as she watched the meeting.

"They say you're going to be in pictures," said Bill Williams.

And then we had Hilda's story over again. Constance asked what papers Mr. Gloster wrote for.

"I don't know. A big paper," said Hilda.

"You ought to find out," Constance said. "I'll find out."

"Um," said Hilda with a nod of not being interested.

"I could give him some of my experience," said Bill Williams. "Couldn't I, Connie? Things I've told you—you could write a ruddy book."

He looked with challenge at Hilda. He was a rival.

"Gawd!" he exclaimed. "The things."

We heard it again, how he was captured, where his battery was, the long march, Sergeant Harris who was hanged, Corporal Rowley bayonetted and left to die in the sun, the starvation, the work on the road that killed half of them. But there was one difference between this story and the ones he had told before. The sight of Hilda altered it.

"You had to get round the guards," he said with a wink. "If you used your loaf a bit, eh? Scrounge around, do a bit of trade. One or two had Japanese girls. Corporal Jones went back afterwards trying to trace his, wanted to marry her."

Hilda listened and talked about places she had lived in, how she had worked in a factory.

38

"That's it," said Bill Williams, "you had to know your way around and talk a bit of the lingo."

Jack Draper looked with affection and wonder at the talk, lowering his eyes if her eyes caught his. Every word entered him. The heat! she said. The rain. The flowers. The telegraph poles! Jack nodded.

"They got telegraph poles." He nodded to us.

You sleep on the floor. Shinji's mother, she mentioned. She could have skinned her. Jack, brought up among so many women, lost interest, but it revived when she talked of Shinji. You could see him mouthing his early marvelling sentence: "She married a Nip," but not saying it. She was confirming something he had often thought of in Normandy; the men on the other side were married too. A bloody marvel. Why hadn't she brought him home? He would have had a friend.

"Who looked after the garden when Shinji was called up?" he asked. "Were they goldfish, ordinary goldfish, in the pond?"

Young Mrs. Draper shook her head. "Eh," she said. "If he'd a known he'd have come over to change the water. Next time we have a war you just let him know."

Mrs. Fulmino, who was throbbing like a volcano, said: "We better all go next time by the sound of it."

At the end, Bill Williams said: "I suppose you're going to be staying here."

"No," said Constance quickly, "she isn't. She's going to France. When is it, Hilda? When is Mr. Gloster coming?"

"Next week, I don't know," said Hilda.

"You shouldn't have let him go!" laughed Bill Williams. "Those French girls will get him in Paree."

"That is what I have been saying," said Constance. "He gave her that brooch."

"Oh, ah! It's the stockings I'm looking at," said Bill Williams. "How did you get all that stuff through the customs? Twenty cases, Connie told me."

"Twelve," said Hilda.

Bill Williams did not move her at all. Presently she got up and started clearing away the tea things. I will say this for her: she didn't let herself be waited on.

Iris, Mr. and Mrs. Fulmino, and the young Drapers and their children and myself left Hincham Street together.

"You walk in front with the children, Iris," said Mrs. Fulmino. Then they turned on me. What was this letter, they wanted to know. Anyone would have thought by their questions that I ought to have opened it and read it.

"I just posted it at the corner." I pointed to the pillar box. Mrs. Fulmino stopped to look at the pillar box and I believe was turning over in her mind the possibility of getting inside it. Then she turned on her husband and said with contemptuous suspicion: "Monte Carlo!" As if he had worked the whole thing in order to go there himself.

"Two dead," she added in her mother's voice, the voice of one who would have been more than satisfied with the death of one.

"Not having a pension hasn't hurt her," said Mrs. Draper.

"Not a tear," said Mrs. Fulmino.

Jack and Mr. Fulmino glanced at each other. It was a glance of surreptitious gratitude: tears—they had escaped that.

Mr. Fulmino said: "The Japanese don't cry."

Mrs. Fulmino stepped out, a bad sign; her temper was rising.

"Who was the letter to?" she asked me. "Was the name Gloster?"

"I didn't look," I said.

Mrs. Fulmino looked at her husband and me and rolled her eyes. Another of our blunders!

"I don't believe it," she said.

But Mrs. Fulmino *did* believe it. We all believed and disbelieved everything at once. I said I would come to the report in the *News*. It was in thick lettering like mourning, with Hilda's picture: A MOTHER'S FAITH. FOUR YEARS IN JAPANESE TORTURE CAMP. LONDON GIRL'S ORDEAL.

And then an account of how Hilda had starved and suffered and been brain-washed by questioners. Even Hilda was awed when she read it, feeling herself drain away, perhaps, and being replaced by this fantasy; and for the rest of us, we had become used to living in a period when events reduced us to beings so trivial that we had no strong feeling of our own existence in relation to the world around us. We had been bashed first one way, then the other, by propaganda, until we were indifferent. At one time people like my parents or old Mrs. Draper could at least trust the sky and feel that it was certain, and before it they could have at least the importance of being something in the eye of heaven.

Constance read the newspaper report and it fulfilled her.

"Propaganda," she said. "Press lies."

"All lies," Mr. Fulmino agreed with wonder. The notion that the untrue was as effective as the true opened to him vast areas to his powers. It was like a temptation.

It did not occur to us that we might be in a difficult situation in the neighbourhood when the truth came out, until we heard Constance and Bill Williams had gone over to the Lord Nelson with the paper and Constance had said: "You can't believe a word you read in the capitalist press."

Alfred Levy, the proprietor and a strong Tory, agreed with her. But was Hilda criticized for marrying an enemy? The hatred of the Japanese was strong at this time. She was not. Constance may not have had the best motives for spreading the news, we said, but it did no harm at all. That habit of double vision affected everyone publicly. We lived in the true and the untrue, comfortably and without trouble. People picked up the paper, looked at her picture, and said: "That's a shocking thing. A British subject," and even when they knew, even from Hilda's own lips, the true story, they said, congratulating themselves on their cunning: "The papers make it all up."

Of course, we were all in that stage where the forces of life, the desire to live, were coming back, and although it was not yet openly expressed, we felt that curiosity about the enemy that ex-soldiers like Jack Draper felt when he wondered if some Japanese or some Germans were as fed up as he was on Saturdays by missing a day's fishing. When people shook Hilda's hand they felt they gave her life. I do not say there were not one or two mutterings afterwards, for people always went off from the Lord Nelson when it closed in a state of moralization: beer must talk; the louts singing and the couples saying this or that "wasn't right." But this gossip came to nothing because, sooner or later, it came to a closed door in everybody's conscience.

There were the men who had shot off trigger fingers, who had got false medical certificates, deserters, ration frauds, black-marketeers, the pilferers of army stores. And the women said a woman is right to stand by her husband and, looking at Hilda's fine clothes, pointed out to their husbands that that kind of loyalty was sometimes rewarded. Mrs. Fulmino, indeed, asserted it ought to be—by law.

We had been waiting for Hilda; now, by a strange turn, we were waiting for Hilda's Mr. Gloster. We waited for a fortnight and it ran on into three weeks. George Hartman Gloster. I looked up the name on our cards at the library, but we had no books of his. I looked up one or two catalogues. Still nothing. It was not surprising. He was an American who was not published in this country. Constance came in and looked too.

"It is one of those names the Americans don't list," she said. Constance smiled with the cool air of keeping a world of meaningful secrets on ice.

"They don't list everything," she said.

She brought Bill Williams with her. I don't think he had ever been in a public library before, because his knowing manner went and he was overawed. He said to me:

"Have you read all these books? Do you buy them second-hand? What's this lot worth?"

He was a man always on the look-out for a deal; it was typical of him that he had come with Constance in his firm's light-green van. It was not like Constance to travel in that way. "Come on," he said roughly.

The weather was hot; we had the sun blinds down in the library. We were in the middle of one of those brassy fort-nights of the London summer when English life as we usually know it is at a standstill, and everyone changes. A new, grinning, healthy race, with long red necks sticking out of open shirts and blouses, appears and the sun brings out the variety of faces and bodies. Constance might have been some trim nurse marching at the head of an official procession. People looked calm, happy, and open. There was hardly ever a cloud in the sky, the slate roofs looked like steel with the sun's rays hitting them, and the side streets were cool in sharp shadow. It was a pleasant time for walking, especially when the sky went whitish in the distances of the city in the evening and when the streets had a dry, pleasant smell and the glass of millions of windows had a motionless but not excluding stare. Even a tailor working late above a closed shop looked pleased to be going on working, while everyone else was out, wearing out their clothes.

Iris and I used to go to the park on some evenings, and there every blade of grass had been wire-brushed by sunlight; the trees were heavy with still leaves, and when darkness came they gathered into soft black walls and their edges were cut out against the nail varnish of the city's night. During the day the park was crowded. All over the long sweeps of grass the couples were lying, their legs at careless angles, their bottoms restless as they turned to the horseplay of love in the open. Girls were leaning over the men rumpling their hair, men were tickling the girls' chins with stalks of grass. Occasionally they would knock the wind out of each other with plunging kisses; and every now and then a girl would sit up and straighten her skirt at the waist, narrowing her eyes in a pretence of looking at some refining sight in the distance, until she was pulled down again and,

44

keeping her knees together, was caught again. Lying down, you smelt the grass and listened to the pleasant rumble of the distant traffic going round like a wheel that never stopped.

I was glad to know the Fulminos and to go out with Iris. We had both been gayer before we met each other, but seriousness, glumness, a sadness came over us when we became friends—that eager sadness that begins with thoughts of love. We encouraged and discouraged these thoughts in each other yet were always hinting, and the sight of so much love around us turned us naturally away from it to think about it privately the more. She was a beautifully formed girl, as her mother must have once been, but slender. She had a wide laugh that shook the curls of her thick black hair. She was being trained at a typing school.

One day when I was sitting in the park and Iris was lying beside me, we had a quarrel. I asked her if there was any news of Mr. Gloster—for she heard everything. She had said there was none and I said, sucking a piece of grass:

"That's what I would like to do. Go round the world. Anywhere. America, Africa, China."

"A chance is a fine thing," said Iris, day-dreaming.

"I could get a job," I said.

Iris sat up. "Leave the Library?" she said.

"Yes," I said. "If I stay there I won't see anything." I saw Iris's face change and become very like her mother's. Mrs. Fulmino could make her face go larger and her mouth go very small. Iris did not answer. I went on talking. I asked her what she thought. She still did not answer.

"Anything the matter?" She was sulking. Then she said, flashing at me:

45

"You're potty on that woman too. You all are. Dad is, Jack is—and look at Bill Williams. Round at Hincham Street every day. He'll be having his breakfast there soon. Fascinated."

"He goes to see Constance."

"Have you seen Constance's face?" she jeered. "Constance could kill her."

"She came to the Library."

"Ah." She turned to me. "You didn't tell me that."

"She came in for a book, I told you. For Mr. Gloster's books. Bill Williams came with her."

Iris's sulk changed into satisfaction at this piece of news.

"Mother says if Constance's going to marry a man like Mrs. Williams," she said, "she'll be a fool to let him out of her sight.

"I'll believe in Mr. Gloster when I see him," Iris said. It was, of course, what we were all thinking. We made up our quarrel and I took Iris home. Mrs. Fulmino was dressed up, just putting the key in the door of her house. Iris was astonished to see her mother had been out and asked where she had been.

"Out," said Mrs. Fulmino. "Have I got to stay in and cook and clean for you all day?"

Mrs. Fulmino was even wearing gloves, as if she had been to church. And she was wearing a new pair of shoes. Iris went pale at the sight of them. Mrs. Fulmino put her gloves down on the sitting-room table and said:

"I've got a right to live, I suppose?"

We were silenced.

One thing we all agreed on while we waited for Mr. Gloster was that Hilda had the money and knew how to

46

spend it. The first time she asked the Fulminos and young
Drapers to the cinema, Mrs. Fulmino said to her husband:

"You go. I've got one of my heads."

"Take Jack," young Mrs. Draper said. "I've got the children."

They were daring their husbands to go with her. But
the second time, there was a party. Hilda took some of them
down to Kew. She took old Mrs. Johnson down to Southend—and who should they meet there but Bill Williams,
who was delivering some goods there, spoiling their day,
because old Mrs. Johnson did not like his ways. And
Hilda had given them all presents. And two or three
nights a week she was out at the Lord Nelson.

It was a good time. If anyone asked: "Have you heard
from Mr. Gloster yet?" Hilda answered that it was not time
yet, and as a dig at Constance which we all admired, she
said once: "He has business at the American Embassy." And
old Mrs. Johnson held her head high and nodded.

At the end of three weeks we became restless. We
noticed old Mrs. Johnson looked poorly. She said she was
tired. Old Mrs. Draper became morose. She had been taught
to call Mr. Gloster by his correct name, but now she relapsed.

"Where is this Indian?" she uttered.

And another day, she said, without explanation:

"Three."

"Three what, Gran?"

"There've been two, that's enough."

No one liked this, but Mrs. Johnson understood.

"Mr. Gloster's very well, isn't he, Hil? You heard from
him yesterday?" she said.

"I wasn't shown the letter," said old Mrs. Draper. "We don't want a third."

"We don't," said Mrs. Fulmino. With her joining in "on Gran's side," the situation changed. Mrs. Fulmino had a low voice and the sound of it often sank to the floor of any room she was in, travelling under chairs and tables, curling round your feet, and filling the place from the bottom as if it were a cistern. Even when the trolley bus went by, Mrs. Fulmino's low voice prevailed. It was an undermining voice, breaking up one's uppermost thoughts and stirring up what was underneath them. It stirred us all now. Yes, we wanted to say, indeed, we wanted to shout, where is this Mr. Gloster, why hasn't he come, did you invent him? He's alive, we hope? Or is he also, as Gran suggests, dead?

Even Mr. Fulmino was worried. "Have you got his address?" he asked.

"Yes, Uncle dear," said Hilda. "He'll be staying at the Savoy. He always does."

Mr. Fulmino had not taken out his notebook for a long time, but he did so now. He wrote down the name.

"Has he made a reservation?" said Mr. Fulmino. "I'll find out if he's booked."

"He hasn't," said Bill Williams. "I had a job down there and I asked. Didn't I, Connie?"

Mrs. Fulmino went a very dark colour; she wished she had thought of doing this. Hilda was not offended, but a small smile clipped her lips as she glanced at Connie.

"I asked Bill to do it," she said.

And then Hilda, in that harsh, lazy voice which she had always used for announcements:

48

"If he doesn't come by Wednesday you'll have to speak for me at your factory, Mrs. Williams. I don't know why he hasn't come, but I can't wait any more."

"Bill can't get you a job. You have to register," said Constance.

"Yes, she'll have to do that," said Mr. Fulmino.

"I'll fix it. Leave it to me," said Bill Williams.

"I expect," said young Mrs. Draper, "his business has kept him." She was sorry for Hilda.

"Perhaps he's gone fishing," said Jack Draper, laughing loudly in a kind way. No one joined in.

"Fishing for orders," said Bill Williams.

Hilda shrugged her shoulders and then she made one of those remarks that Grandma Draper usually made: I suppose the gift really ran through the family.

"Perhaps it was a case," she said, "of ships that pass in the night."

"Oh no, dear," said Mrs. Johnson, trembling, "not ships." We went to the bus stop afterwards with the Fulminos and the Johnsons. Mrs. Fulmino's calm had gone. She marched out first, her temper rising.

"Ships!" she said. "When you think of what we went through during the war. Did you hear her? Straight out?"

"My brother Herbert's wife was like that. She's a widow. Take away the pension and they'll work like the rest of us. I had to."

"Job! Work! I know what sort of work she's been doing. Frank, walk ahead with Iris."

"Well," said young Mrs. Draper. "She won't be able to go to work in those clothes and that's a fact."

49

"All show," said Mrs. Fulmino triumphantly. "And I'll tell you something else: she hasn't a penny. She's run through her poor mother's money."

"Ay, I don't doubt," said young Mrs. Draper, who had often worked out how much the old lady had saved.

Mrs. Gloster did not come on Wednesday or on any day, but Hilda did not get a job either, not at once. And old Mrs. Johnson did not go to Monte Carlo. She died. This was the third, we understood, that old Mrs. Draper had foreseen.

Mrs. Johnson died at half past eight in the morning just after Constance had gone off to school, the last day of the term, and before old Mrs. Draper had got up. Hilda was in the kitchen wearing her blue Japanese wrap when she heard her mother's loud shout, like a man selling papers, she said, and when Hilda rushed in, her mother was sitting up in bed. She gripped Hilda with the ferocity of the dying, as if all the strength of her whole life had come back and she was going to throw her daughter to the ground. Then she died. In an hour she looked like a white leaf that has been found after a lifetime pressed between the pages of a book and as delicate as a saint. The death was not only a shock; from the grief that spread from it staining all of us, I trace the ugly events that followed. Only the frail figure of old Mrs. Johnson, with her faith and her sly smile, had protected us from them until then, and when she went, all defence went with her.

I need not describe her funeral: it was done by Bickerson's; Mr. Fulmino arranged it. But one thing astonished us: not only our families but the whole neighbourhood was affected by the death of this woman who, in our carelessness, we thought could hardly be known to anyone. She had lived there all her life, of course, but people come and go in London; only a sluggish residue stay still; and I believe it was just because a large number of passing people knew just a little about her, because she was a fragment in their minds, that her death affected them. They recognized that they themselves were not people but fragments. People remembered her going into shops now and then, or going down to the bus stop, passing down a street. They remembered the bag of American cloth she used to carry containing her sewing; they spoke for a long time afterwards about this bag, more about it, indeed, than about herself. Bickerson's is a few doors from the Lord Nelson, so that when the hearse stood there covered with flowers, everyone noticed it, and although the old lady had not been in that public house for years since the death of her husband, all the customers came out to look. And they looked at Hilda sitting in her black in the car when the hearse moved slowly off, and all who knew her story must have felt that the dream was burying the dreamer. Hilda's face was dirty with grief and she did not turn her head to right or left as they drove off. I remember a small thing that happened when we were all together at old Mrs. Draper's, after we had got her back with difficulty up the stairs.

"Bickerson's did it very well," said Mr. Fulmino, seeking to distract the old lady, who, swollen with sadness, was uncomfortable in her best clothes. "They organize everything so well. They gave me this."

He held up a small brass disc on a little chain. It was one of those identity discs people used to wear on their wrists in the war.

"She had never taken it off," he said. It swung feebly on its chain. Suddenly, with a sound like a shout, Mr. Fulmino broke into tears. His face caved in and he apologized.

"It's the feeling," he said. "You have the feeling. You feel." And he looked at us with panic, astonished by this discovery of an unknown self, spongy with tears, that had burst out and against which he was helpless. Mrs. Fulmino said gently: "I expect Hilda would like to have it."

"Yes, yes. It's for her," he said, drying his eyes, and Hilda took it from him and carried it to her room. While she was there (and perhaps she was weeping, too), Mr. Fulmino looked out from his handkerchief and said, still sobbing:

"I see that the luggage has gone."

None of us had noticed this and we looked at Constance, who said in a whisper: "She is leaving us. She has found a room of her own." That knocked us back. "Leaving!" we exclaimed. It told against Hilda, for although we talked of death being a release for the dead person, we did not like to think of it as a release for the living; grief ought to hold people together, and it seemed too brisk to have started a new life so soon. Constance alone looked pleased by this. We were whispering but stopped when we heard Hilda coming back.

Black had changed her. It set off her figure, and although crying had hardened her, the skin of her neck and her arms and the swell of her breasts seemed more living than they had before. She looked stronger in body perhaps because she was shaken in mind. She looked very real, very present,

52

more alive than ourselves. She had not heard us whispering, but she said, to all of us, but particularly to Mr. Fulmino:

"I have found a room for myself. Constance spoke to Bill Williams for me: he's good at getting things. He found me a place and he took the luggage round yesterday. I couldn't sleep in that bed alone any more."

Her voice was shaky.

"She didn't take up much room. She was tiny and we managed. It was like sleeping with a little child."

Hilda smiled and laughed a little.

"She used to kick like a kid."

Ten minutes on the bus from Hincham Street and close to the centre of London is a dance hall called the Temple Rooms. It has two bands, a low gallery where you can sit, and a soft drink bar. Quite a few West Indians go there, mainly students. It is a respectable place; it closes at eleven and there is never any trouble. Iris and I went there once or twice. One evening we were surprised to see Constance and Bill Williams dancing there. Iris pointed to them. The rest of the people were jiving, but Bill Williams and Constance were dancing in the old-fashioned way.

"Look at his feet!" Iris laughed.

Bill Williams was paying no attention to Constance, but looking round the room over her head as he stumbled along. He was tall.

"Fancy Auntie Constance!" said Iris. "She's getting fed-up because he won't listen."

Constance Draper dancing! At her age! Thirty-eight!

"It's since the funeral," said Mr. Fulmino over our usual cup of tea. "She was fond of the old lady. It's upset her."

When My Girl Comes Home

Even I knew Mr. Fulmino was wrong about this. The madness of Constance dated from the time Bill Williams had taken Hilda's luggage round to her room and got her a job at the reception desk in the factory at Laxton. It dated from the time, a week later, when, standing at old Mrs. Draper's early one evening, Constance had seen Hilda get out of Bill Williams's van. He had given her a lift home. It dated from words that passed between Hilda and Constance soon afterwards. Hilda said Williams hung round for her at the factory and wanted her to go to a dance. She did not want to go, she said, and here came the fatal sentences—both of her husbands had been educated men. Constance kept her temper but said coldly:

"Bill Williams is politically educated."

Hilda had her vacant look. "Not his hands aren't," she said.

The next thing, Constance, who hardly went into a pub in her life, was in the Lord Nelson night after night, playing bar billiards with Bill Williams. She never let him out of her sight. She came out of school and instead of going home, marking papers, and getting a meal for herself and old Mrs. Draper, she took the bus out to the factory and waited for him to come out. Sometimes he had left on some job by the time she got there and she came home, beside herself, questioning everybody. It had been her habit to come twice a week to change her library books. Now she did not come. She stopped reading. At the Temple Rooms, when Iris and I saw her, she sat out holding hands with Bill Williams and rubbing her head into his shoulder, her eyes watching him the whole time. We went to speak to them and Constance asked:

"Is Hilda here tonight?"

"I haven't seen her."

"She's a whore," said Constance in a loud voice. We thought she was drunk.

It was a funny thing, Mr. Fulmino said to me, to call a woman a whore. He spoke as one opposed to funny things.

"If they'd listened to me," he said, "I could have stopped all this trouble. I offered to get her a job in the Council office, but"—he rolled his eyes—"Mrs. F. wouldn't have it, and while we were arguing about it, Bill Williams acts double quick. It's all because this Mr. Gloster didn't turn up."

Mr. Fulmino spoke wistfully. He was, he conveyed, in the middle of a family battle; indeed, he had a genuine black eye the day we talked about this. Mrs. Fulmino's emotions were in her arms.

This was a bad period for Mr. Fulmino because he had committed a folly. He had chosen this moment to make a personal triumph. He had got himself promoted to a much better job at the Council offices and one entitling him to a pension. He had become a genuine official. To have promoted a man who had the folly to bring home a rich whore with two names, so causing the robbery and death of her mother, and to have let her break Constance's heart was, in Mrs. Fulmino's words, a crime. Naturally, Mr. Fulmino regarded his mistakes as mere errors of routine and even part of his training for his new position.

"Oh well," he said when we finished our tea and got up to pay the bill. "It's the British taxpayer that pays." He was heading for politics. I have heard it said, years later, that if he had had a better start in life he would have gone to the top of the administration. It is a tragic calling.

If Hilda was sinister to Constance and Mrs. Fulmino, she made a different impression on young Mrs. Draper. To call a woman a whore was neither here nor there to her. Up north where she came from, people were saying that sort of thing all day long as they scrubbed floors or cleaned windows or did the washing. The word gave them energy and made things come up cleaner and whiter. Good money was earned hard; easy money went easy. To young Mrs. Draper, Hilda seemed "a bit simple," but she had gone to work, she earned her living. Cut off from the rest of the Draper family, Hilda made friends with this couple. Hilda went with them on Saturday to the zoo with the children. They were looking at a pair of monkeys. One of them was dozing and its companion was awake, pestering and annoying it. The children laughed. But when they moved on to another cage, Hilda said, sulkily:

"That's one thing. Bill Williams won't be here. He pesters me all the time."

"He won't if you don't let him," said young Mrs. Draper.

"I'm going to give my notice if he doesn't stop," said Hilda. She hunched a shoulder and looked round at the animals.

"I can't understand a girl like Constance taking up with him. He's not on her level. And he's mean. He doesn't give her anything. I asked if he gave her that clip, but she said it was Gran's. Well, if a man doesn't give you anything he doesn't value you. I mean she's a well-read girl."

"There's more ways than one of being stupid," said young Mrs. Draper.

"I wonder she doesn't see," said Hilda. "He's not delivering for the firm. When he's got the van out, he's doing some-

56

thing on the side. When I came home with him, there was stuff at the back. And he keeps on asking how much things cost. He offered to sell my bracelet."

"You'd get a better price in a shop if you're in need," said young Mrs. Draper.

"She'd better not be with him if he gets stopped on the road," said Jack, joining in. "You wouldn't sell that. Your husband gave it you."

"No. Mr. Faulkner," said Hilda, pulling out her arm and admiring it.

Jack was silent and disappointed; then he cheered up. "You ought to have married that earl you were always talking about when you were a girl. Do you remember?" he said.

"Earls—they're a lazy lot," said young Mrs. Draper.

"I did, Jack," said Hilda. "They were as good as earls, both of them."

And to young Mrs. Draper she said: "They wouldn't let another man look at me. I felt like a woman with both of them."

"I've nowt against that if you've got the time," said young Mrs. Draper. She saw that Hilda was glum.

"Let's go back and look at the giraffes. Perhaps Mrs. Faulkner will come for you now Mr. Gloster hasn't," young Mrs. Draper said.

"They were friends," said Hilda.

"Oh, they knew each other!" said young Mrs. Draper. "I thought you just . . . met them. . . ."

"No, I didn't meet them together, but they were friends."

"Yes. Jack had a friend, didn't you?" said Mrs. Draper, remembering.

"That's right," said Jack. He winked at Hilda. "Neck and neck, it was." And then he laughed outright.

"I remember something about Bill Williams. He came out with us one Saturday and you should have seen his face when we threw the fish back in the water."

"We always throw them back," said young Mrs. Draper, taking her husband's arm, proudly.

"Wanted to sell them or something. Black-market perch!"

"He thinks I've got dollars," said Hilda.

"No, fancy, Jack—Mr. Gloster and Mr. Faulkner being friends. Well, that's nice."

And she looked sentimentally at Hilda.

"She's brooding," young Mrs. Draper said to Mrs. Fulmino after this visit to the zoo. "She won't say anything." Mrs. Fulmino said she had better not or *she* might say something. "She knows what I think. I never thought much of Bill Williams, but he served his country. She didn't."

"She earns her living," said Mrs. Draper.

"Like we all do," said Mrs. Fulmino. "And it's not men, men, men all day long with you and me."

"One's enough," said young Mrs. Draper, "with two children round your feet."

"She doesn't come near me," said Mrs. Fulmino.

"No," Mr. Fulmino said sadly, "after all we've done."

They used to laugh at me when I went dancing with Iris at the Temple Rooms. We had not been there for more than a month and Iris said:

"He can't stop staring at the band."

She was right. The beams of the spotlights put red, green, violet, and orange tents on the hundreds of dancers. It was like the Arabian nights. When we got there, Ted Custer's band was already at it like cats on dustbins and tearing their guts out. The pianist had a very thin neck and kept wagging his head as if he were ga-ga; if his head had fallen off he would have caught it in one of his crazy hands and popped it on again without losing a note; the trumpet player had thick eyebrows that went higher and higher as he tried and failed to burst; the drummers looked doped; the saxophone went at it like a man in bed with a girl who had purposely left the door open. I remember them all, especially the thin-lipped man, very white-faced, with the double bass drawing his bow at knee level, to and fro, slowly, sinful. They all whispered, nodded, and rocked together, telling dirty stories until bang, bang, bang, the dancers went faster and faster, the row hit the ceiling or died out with the wheeze of a balloon. I was entranced.

"Don't look as though you're going to kill someone," Iris said.

That shows how wrong people are. I was full of love and wanted to cry.

After four dances I went off to the soft-drink bar and there the first person I saw was Bill Williams. He was wearing a plum-coloured suit and a red and silver tie and he stood, with his dark hair, dusty-looking and spouting forward as if he had just got out of bed and was ducking his head on the way to the lavatory.

"All the family here?" he asked, looking all round.

"No," I said. "Just Iris and me."

He went on looking round him.

"I thought you only came Saturdays," he said suspiciously. He had a couple of friends with him, two men who became restless on their feet, as if they were dancing, when I came up.

"Oh," said Bill Williams. Then he said: "Nicky pokey doda—that's Japanese, pal, for 'keep your mouth shut.' Anyone say anything, you never see me. I'm at Laxton, get me? Bill Williams? He's on night shift. You must be barmy. Okay? Seeing you," he said. "No sign of Connie."

And he walked off. His new friends went a step or two after him, dancing on their pointed shoes, and then stopped. They twizzled round, tapping their feet, looking all round the room until he had got to the carpeted stairs at the end of the hall. I got my squash, and when I turned round, the two men too had gone.

But before Bill Williams had got to the top of the stairs he turned round to look at the dancers in one corner. There was Hilda. She was dancing with a young West Indian. When I got back to our table she was very near.

I have said that Hilda's face was eventless. It was now in a tranced state, looking from side to side, to the floor, in the quick turns of the dance, swinging round, stepping back, stepping forward. The West Indian had a long jacket on. His knees were often nearly bent double as though he were going to do some trick of crawling towards her; then he recovered himself and turned his back as if he had never met her and was dancing with someone else. If Hilda's face was eventless, it was the event itself, it was the dance.

She saw us when the dance was over and came to our table breathlessly. She was astonished to see us. To me she said: "And fancy you!" She did not laugh or even smile when she looked at me. I don't know how to describe her look. It was dead. It had no expression. It had nothing. Or rather, by the smallest twitch of a muscle, it became nothing. Her face had the nakedness of a body. She saw that I was deaf to what Iris was saying. Then she smiled, and in doing that, she covered herself.

"I am with friends over there"—we could not tell who the friends were—and then she leaned towards us and whispered:

"Bill Williams is here, too."

Iris exclaimed.

"He's watching me," Hilda said.

"I saw him," I said. "He's gone."

Hilda stood up, frowning. "Are you sure? Did you see him? How long ago?"

I said it was about five minutes before.

She stood as I remember her standing in Mrs. Draper's room on the first day when she arrived and was kissing everyone. It was a peculiar stance because she usually stood so passively; a stance of action and, I now saw, a stance of plain fright. One leg was planted forward and bent at the knee like a runner at the start and one arm was raised and bent at the elbow, the elbow pushed out beyond her body. Her mouth was open and her deep-set yellow eyes seemed to darken and look tired.

"He was with some friends," I said, and, looking back at the bar: "They've gone now."

"Hah!" It was the sound of a gasp of breath. Then suddenly the fright went and she shrugged her shoulders and talked and laughed to all of us. Soon she went over to her friends, the coloured man and a white couple; she must have got some money or the ticket for her handbag from one of them, for presently we saw her walking quickly to the cloakroom.

Iris went on dancing. We must have stayed another half an hour, and when we were leaving we were surprised to see Hilda waiting in the foyer. She said to me:

"His car has gone."

"Whose?"

"Bill Williams's car."

"Has he got a car?" Iris said.

"Oh, it's not his," said Hilda. "It's gone. That's something. Will you take me home? I don't want to go alone. They followed me here."

She looked at all of us. She was frightened.

I said: "Iris and I will take you on our way."

"Don't make me late," said Iris crossly. "You know what Mum is." I promised. "Did you come with him?"

"No, with someone else," Hilda said, looking nervously at the revolving glass door. "Are you sure his friends went too? What did they look like?"

I tried to describe them.

"I've seen the short one," she said, frowning, "somewhere."

It was only a quarter of an hour's ride at that hour of the night. We walked out of the Temple Rooms and across the main road to the bus stop and waited under the lights that made our faces corpse-like. I have always liked the hard and sequined sheen of London streets at night, their empty-dockyard look. The cars come down them like rats. The red trolley bus came up at last, and when we got in, Hilda sat between us. The busload of people stared at her and I

62

am not surprised. I have not said what she looked like—the hair built up high, her bright-green wrap and red dress. I don't know how you would describe such clothes. But the people were not staring at her clothes. They were staring at her eyebrows. I said before that her face was an extension of her nakedness. I say it again. Those eyebrows of hers were painted and looked like the only things she had on; they were like a pair of beetles with turned-up tails that had settled on her forehead. People laughed behind their hands and two or three youths at the front of the bus turned round and guffawed and jostled and whistled; but Hilda, remember, was not a girl of sixteen gone silly, but a woman, hard rather than soft in the face, and the effect was one of exposure, just as a mask has the effect of exposing. We did not talk, but when the trolley arm thumped two or three times at a street junction, Hilda said with a sigh: "Bump! Bump! Bump!." She was thinking of her childhood in old Mrs. Draper's room at Hincham Street. We got off the bus a quarter of a mile further on, and as she was stepping off, Hilda said, speaking of what was in her mind, I suppose, during the ride:

"Shinji had a gold wrist watch with a gold strap and a golden pen. They had gone when he was killed. They must have cost him a hundred pounds. Someone must have stolen them and sold them.

"I reported it," Hilda said. "I needed the money. That is what you had to do—sell. Everything. I had to eat."

And the stare from her mask of a face stated something of her life that her strangeness had concealed from us. We walked up the street.

She went on talking about that watch and how particular

63

Shinji was about his clothes, especially his shirts. All his collars had to be starched, she said. Those had gone too, she said. And his glasses. And his two gold rings. She walked very quickly between us. We got to the corner of her street. She stopped and looked down it.

"Bill Williams's van!" she said.

About thirty houses down the street we could indeed see a small van standing.

"He's waiting for me," she said.

It was hard to know whether she was frightened or whether she was reckoning, but my heart jumped. She made us stand still and watch. "My room's in the front," she said. I crossed over to the other side of the street and then came back.

"The light is on," I said.

"He's inside," she said.

"Shall I go and see?" I said.

"Go," said Iris to me.

Hilda held my wrist. "No," she said.

"There are two people, I think, in the front garden," I said.

"I'm going home with you," Hilda said to Iris decisively. She rushed off and we had to race after her. We crossed two or three streets to the Fulminos' house. Mrs. Fulmino let us in.

"Now, now, Hilda, keep your hair on. Kill you? Why should he? This is England, this isn't China. . . ."

Mr. Fulmino's face showed his agony. His mouth collapsed, his eyes went hard. He looked frantic with appeal. Then he turned his back on us, marched into the parlour,

64

and shouted as if he were calling across four lines of traffic:

"Turn the wireless off."

We followed him into the room. Mrs. Fulmino, in the suddenly silent room, looked like a fortress waiting for a flag to fall.

We all started talking at once.

"Can I stay with you tonight?" she said. "Bill Williams has broken into my house. I can't go there. He'll kill me." The flag fell.

"Japan," said Mrs. Fulmino, disposing of her husband with her first shot. Then she turned to Hilda; her voice was coldly rich and rumbling. "You've always a home here, as you well know, Hilda," she went on, giving a very unhomely sound to the word. "And," she said, glancing at her neat curtains, to anyone who might be in ambush outside the window, "if anyone tries to kill you, they will have to kill"—she nodded to her husband—"Ted and me first. What have you been doing?"

"I was down at the Temple. Not with Bill Williams," said Hilda. "He was watching me. He's always watching me."

"Now, look here, Hilda, why should Bill Williams want to kill you? Have you encouraged him?"

"Don't be a fool," shouted Mrs. Fulmino.

"She knows what I mean. Listen to me, Hilda. What's going on between you and Bill Williams? Constance is upset, we all know."

"Oh, keep your big mouth shut," said Mrs. Fulmino. "Of course she's encouraged him. Hilda's a woman, isn't she? I encouraged you, didn't I?"

"I know how to look after myself," said Hilda, "but I don't like that van outside the house at this hour of night. I didn't speak to him at the dance."

"Hilda's thinking of the police," ventured Mr. Fulmino.

"Police!" said Mrs. Fulmino. "Do you know what's in the van?"

"No," said Hilda. "And that's what I don't want to know. I don't want him on my doorstep. Or his friends. He had two with him. Harry saw them."

Mrs. Fulmino considered.

"I'm glad you've come to us. I wish you'd come to us in the first place," she said. Then she commanded Mr. Fulmino: "You go up there at once with Harry," she said, "and tell that man to leave Hilda alone. Go on, now. I can't understand you"—she indicated me—"running off like that, leaving a van there. If you don't go, I'll go myself. I'm not afraid of a paltry . . . a paltry . . . What does he call himself? You go up."

Mrs. Fulmino was as good a judge of the possibilities of an emotional situation as any woman on earth: this was her moment. She wanted us out of the house and Hilda to herself.

We obeyed.

Mr. Fulmino and I left the house. He looked tired. He was too tired to put on his jacket. He went out in his shirt sleeves.

"Up and down we go, in and out, up and down," said Mr. Fulmino. "First it's Constance, now it's Hilda. And the pubs are closed."

"There you are, what did I tell you?" said Mr. Fulmino when we got to Hilda's street. "No van, no sign of it, is

66

there? You're a witness. We'll go up and see, all the same."

Mr. Fulmino had been alarmed, but now his confidence came back. He gave me a wink and a nod when we got to the house.

"Leave it to me," he said. "You wait here."

I heard him knock at the door and after a time knock again. Then I heard a woman's voice. He was talking a long time. He came away.

He was silent for a long time as we walked. At last he said:

"That beats all. I didn't say anything. I didn't say who I was. I didn't let on. I just asked to see Hilda. 'Oh,' says the landlady, 'she's out.' 'Oh,' I said, 'that's a surprise.' I didn't give a name. 'Out, you say? When will she be back?' 'I don't know,' said the landlady, and this is it, Harry—'she's paid her rent and given her notice. She's leaving first thing in the morning,' the landlady said. 'They came for the luggage this evening.' Harry," said Mr. Fulmino, "did Hilda say anything about leaving?"

"No."

"Bill Williams came for her luggage."

We marched on. Or rather we went stealthily along like two men walking a steel wire of suspicion. We almost lost our balance when two cats ran across the street and set up howls in a garden, as if they were howling us down. Mr. Fulmino stopped.

"Harry!" he said. "She's playing us up. She's going off with Bill Williams."

"But she's frightened of him. She said he was going to kill her."

"I'm not surprised," said Mr. Fulmino. "She's been playing him up. Who was she with at the dance hall? She's played everyone up. Of course she's frightened of him. You bet. I'm sorry for anyone getting mixed up with Bill Williams: he'll knock some sense into her. He's rough. So was her father."

"Bill Williams might have just dropped by to have a word," I said.

Mr. Fulmino marched forward again.

"Funny word at half past eleven at night," said Mr. Fulmino. "When I think of all that correspondence, all those forms—War Office, State Department, United Nations—we did, it's been a poor turn-out. You might say"—he paused for an image sufficiently devastating—"a waste of paper, a ruddy wanton waste of precious paper."

We got back to his house. I have never mentioned I believe that it had an iron gate that howled and a clipped privet hedge like a moustache to the tiny garden.

We opened the gate, the gate howled, Mrs. Fulmino's nose appeared at the curtains.

"Don't say a word," said Mr. Fulmino.

Tea—the room smelt of that, of course. Mrs. Fulmino had made some while we were out. She looked as though she had eaten something, too. A titbit. They all looked sorry for Mr. Fulmino and me. And Mrs. Fulmino *had* had a titbit! In fact I know from Iris that the only thing Mrs. Fulmino had got out of Hilda was the news that she had had a postcard from Mr. Faulkner from Chicago. He was on the move.

"Well?" said Mrs. Fulmino.

"It's all right, Hilda," said Mr. Fulmino coldly. "They've gone."

"There," said Mrs. Fulmino, patting Hilda's hand.

"Hilda," said Mr. Fulmino, "I've been straight with you. I want you to be straight with me. What's going on between you and Bill Williams? . . ."

"Hilda's told me," Mrs. Fulmino said.

"I asked Hilda, not you," said Mr. Fulmino to his wife, who was so surprised that she went very white instead of her usual purple.

"Hilda, come on. You come round here saying he's going to kill you. Then they tell me you've given your notice up there."

"She told me that. I think she's done the right thing."

"And did you tell her why you gave your notice?" asked Mr. Fulmino.

"She's given her notice at the factory, too," said Mrs. Fulmino.

"Why?" said Mr. Fulmino.

Hilda did not answer.

"You are going off with Bill Williams, aren't you?"

"Ted!" Hilda gave one of her rare laughs.

"What's this?" cried Mrs. Fulmino. "Have you been deceiving me? Deceit I can't stand, Hilda."

"Of course she is," said Mr. Fulmino. "She's paid her rent. He's collected her luggage this evening. Where is it to be? Monte Carlo? Oh, it's all right, sit down." Mr. Fulmino waved Mrs. Fulmino back. "They had a row at the dance this evening."

But Hilda was on her feet.

"My luggage!" she cried, holding her bag with both hands to her bosom as we had seen her do once before when she was cornered. "Who has touched my luggage?"

I thought she was going to strike Mr. Fulmino.

"The dirty thief. Who let him in? Who let him take it? Where's he gone?"

She was moving to the door. We were stupefied.

"Bill Williams!" she shouted. Her rage made those artificial eyebrows look comical, and I expected her to pick them off and throw them at us. "Bill Williams, I'm talking about. Who let that bloody war hero in? That bitch up there . . ."

"Hilda," said Mrs. Fulmino. "We don't want language.

"You fool," said Mrs. Fulmino in her lowest, most floor-sweeping voice to her husband. "What have you been and done? You've let Bill Williams get away with all those cases, all her clothes, everything. You let that spiv strip her."

"Go off with Bill Williams!" Hilda laughed. "My husband was an officer."

"I knew he was after something. I thought it was dollars," she said suddenly.

She came back from the door and sat down at the table and sobbed.

"Two hundred and fifty pounds he's got," she sobbed. It was a sight to see Hilda weeping. We could not speak.

"It's all I had," she said.

We watched Hilda. The painted eyebrows made the grimace of her weeping horrible. There was not one of us who was not shocked. There was in all of us a sympathy we knew how to express but that was halted—as by a fascination—with the sight of her ruin. We could not help contrasting her triumphant arrival with her state at this moment. It was as if we had at last got her with us as we had, months before, expected her to be. Perhaps she read our

70

thoughts. She looked up at us and she had the expression of a person seeing us for the first time. It was like an inspection.

"You're a mean lot, a mean respectable lot," she said. "I remember you. I remember when I was a girl. What was it Mr. Singh said? I can't remember—he was clever—oh well, leave it, leave it. When I saw that little room they put my poor mother in, I could have cried. No sun. No warmth in it. You just wanted someone to pity. I remember it. And your faces. The only thing that was nice was"—she sobbed and laughed for a moment—"was bump, bump, bump, the trolley." She said loudly: "There's only one human being in the whole crew—Jack Draper. I don't wonder he sees more in fish."

She looked at me scornfully. "Your brother—he was nice," she said. "Round the park at night! That was love."

"Hilda," said Mrs. Fulmino without anger. "We've done our best for you. If we've made mistakes I hope you haven't. We haven't had your life. You talk about ships that pass in the night. I don't know what you mean, but I can tell you there are no ships in this house. Only Ted."

"That's right," said Mr. Fulmino quietly too. "You're overwrought."

"Father," said Mrs. Fulmino, "hadn't you better tell the police?"

"Yes, yes, dear," agreed Mr. Fulmino. "We'd better get in touch with the authorities."

"Police," said Hilda, laughing in their faces. "Oh, God. Don't worry about that. You've got one in every house in this country." She picked up her bag, still laughing, and went to the door.

"Police," she was saying, "that's ripe."

"Hilda, you're not to go out in the street looking like that," said Mrs. Fulmino.

"I'd better go with her," said Mr. Fulmino.

"I'll go," I said. They were glad to let me.

It is ten years since I walked with Hilda to her lodgings. I shall not forget it, and the warm, dead, rubbery city night. It is frightening to walk with a woman who has been robbed and wronged. Her eyes were half closed as though she was reckoning as she walked. I had to pull her back on to the pavement or she would have gone flat into a passing car. The only thing she said to me was:

"They took Shinji's rings as well."

Her room was on the ground floor. It had a divan and a not very clean dark-green cover on it. A pair of shoes were sticking out from under it. There was a plain deal cupboard and she went straight to it. Two dresses were left. The rest had gone. She went to a table and opened the drawer. It was empty except for some letters.

I stood not knowing what to say. She seemed surprised to see me there still.

"He's cleared the lot," she said vacantly. Then she seemed to realize that she was staring at me without seeing me, for she lowered her angry shoulders.

"We'll get them back," I said.

"How?" she said, mocking me, but not unkindly.

"I will," I said. "Don't be upset."

"You!" she said.

"Yes, I will," I said.

I wanted to say more. I wanted to touch her. But I couldn't. The ruin had made her untouchable.

72

"What are you going to do?" I said.

"Don't worry about me," she said. "I'm okey doke. You're different from your brother. You don't remember those days. I told Mr. Gloster about him. Come to that, Mr. Faulkner too. They took it naturally. That was a fault of Mr. Singh"—she never called him by his Christian name—"jealousy."

She kicked off her shoes and sat down on the cheap divan and frowned at the noise it made and she laughed.

"One day in Bombay I got homesick and he asked me what I was thinking about, and I was green, I just said: 'Sid Fraser's neck. It had a mole on it.' You should have seen his face. He wouldn't talk to me for a week. It's a funny thing about those countries. Some people might rave about them, I didn't see anything to them."

She got up.

"You go now," she said, laughing. "I must have been in love."

I dreamed about Hilda's face all night, and in the morning I wouldn't have been surprised to see London had been burned out to a cinder. But the next night her face did not come and I had to think about it. Further and further it went, a little less every day and night, and I did not seem to notice when someone said Bill Williams had been picked up by the police, or when Constance had been found half dead with aspirins, and when, in both cases, Mr. Fulmino told me he had to "give assistance in the identification," for Hilda had gone. She left the day after I took her to her room. Where she went no one knew. We guessed. We imagined. Across water, I thought, getting further and further away, in very fine clothes and very beautiful.

France, Mr. Fulmino thought, or possibly Italy. Africa, even. New York, San Francisco, Tokyo, Bombay, Singapore. Where? Even one day six months after she had left, when he came to the library and showed me a postcard he had had from her, the first message, it did not say where she was and someone in the post office had pulled off the stamp. It was a picture of Hilda herself on a seat in a park, sitting with Mr. Faulkner and Mr. Gloster. You wouldn't recognize her.

But Mr. Gloster's book came out. Oh yes. It wasn't about Japan or India or anything like that. It was about us.

The Wheelbarrow

R obert," Miss Freshwater's niece called down from the window of the dismantled bedroom, "when you have finished that, would you mind coming upstairs a minute? I want you to move a trunk."

And when Evans waved back from the far side of the rumpled lawn where he was standing by the bonfire, she closed the window to keep out the smoke of slow-burning rubbish—old carpeting, clothes, magazines, papers, boxes —which hung about the waists of the fir trees and blew towards the house. For three days the fire had been burning, and Evans, red-armed in his shirt sleeves and sweating along the seams of his brow, was prodding it with a garden fork. A sudden silly tongue of yellow flame wagged out: some inflammable piece of family history—who knew what? Perhaps one of her aunt's absurd summer hats or a shocking year of her father's day-dream accountancy—was having its last fling. She saw Evans pick up a bit of paper from the outskirts of the fire and read it. What was it? Miss Freshwater's niece drew back her lips and opened her mouth expectantly. At this stage all family privacy had gone. Thirty, forty, fifty years of life were going up in smoke.

75

The Wheelbarrow

Evans took up the wheelbarrow and swaggered back with it across the lawn towards the house, sometimes tipping it a little to one side to see how the rubber-tyred wheel was running and to admire it. Miss Freshwater's niece smiled. With his curly black hair, his sun-reddened face, and his vacant blue eyes, and the faint white scar or chip on the side of his nose, he looked like some hard-living, hard-bitten doll. "Burn this? This lot to go?" was his cry. He was an impassioned and natural destroyer. She could not have found a better man. "Without you, Robert," she said on the first day and with real feeling, "I could never have faced it."

It was pure luck getting him, but, lazy, smiling and drifting, she always fell on her feet. She had stepped off the morning train from London at the beginning of the week and had stood on the curb in the station yard, waiting for one of the two or three taxi drivers who were talking there to take notice of her. Suddenly, Evans drove in fast from the street outside, pulled up beside her, pushed her in, and drove off. It was like an abduction. The other taxi drivers shouted at him in the bad language of law-abiding men, but Evans slowly moved his hand up and down, palm downwards, silently and insultingly telling them to shut up and keep their hair on. He looked very pious as he did this. It made her laugh out loud.

"They are manner-less," he said in a slow, rebuking voice, giving each syllable its clear value as if he were speaking the phrase of a poem. "I am sorry I did not ask you where you want me to take you."

They were going in the wrong direction, and he had to swing round the street. She now saw him glance at her in the mirror and his doll's eyes quickly changed from shrewd pleasure to vacancy: she was a capture.

"This is not the first time you are here, I suppose?" he said.

"I was born here," she said. "I haven't been here for twenty-five years—well, perhaps just for a day a few years ago. It has changed. All this building!"

She liked friendly conversations.

They were driving up the long hill out of the town to-wards her aunt's house. Once there had been woodland here but now, like a red hard sea flowing in to obliterate her memory, thousands of sharp villas replaced the trees in angular waves.

"Yes," he said simply. "There is money everywhere."

The car hummed up the long, concrete hill. The villas gave way to ribbons of shacks and bungalows. The gardens were buzzing with June flowers. He pointed out a bunga-low that had a small grocery shop in the lean-to at the side, a yard where a couple of old cars stood, and a petrol pump. That was his place, he said. And then, beyond that, were the latest municipal housing estates built close to the Green, which was only half a mile from her aunt's house. As they passed, she saw a white marquee on the Green and a big sagging white banner with the words "Gospel Mission" daubed on it.

"I see the Gospellers still keep it up," she said. For it was all bad land outside the town, a place for squatters, poor craftsmen, smallholders, little men with little sheds, who in their flinty way had had for generations the habit of break-ing out into little religious sects.

77

"Oh, yes," said Evans in a soft voice, shocked that she could doubt it. "There are great openings. There is a mighty coming to the Lord. I toil in the vineyard myself. You are Miss Freshwater's niece?" he said. "She was a toiler too. She was a giantess for the Lord."

She saw she had been reckless in laughing. She saw she was known. It was as if he had knowingly captured her.

"You don't come from these parts, do you?" she said.

"I am from Wales," he said. "I came here from the mines. I ob-ject-ed to the starvation."

They arrived at the ugly yellow house. It could hardly be seen through the overgrown laurels and fir trees which in some places fingered the dirty windows. He steadied her as she got out, for she had put on weight in the last year or so, and while she opened her bag to find some money, he walked to the gate and looked in.

"It was left to you in the will, I suppose?" he said.

"Yes," she said. She was a woman always glad to confide. "I've come down to clear up the rubbish before the sale. Do you know anyone here who would give me a hand?"

"There are many," he pronounced. "They are too handy." It was like a line from an anthem. He went ahead, opened the gate, and led the way in, and when she opened the front door, splitting it away from the cobwebs, he went in with her, walking into the stale, sun-yellowed rooms. He looked up the worn carpet of the stairs. He looked at the ceilings, measuring the size of everything.

"It will fetch a high price," he said in a sorrowful voice and then, looking over her figure like a farmer at the market, in case she might go with the property, he added enthusiasm to his sorrow.

"The highest!" he said. "Does this door go to the back?"
She lost him for a while. When she found him he was outside, at the back of the house, looking into sheds. He had
opened the door of one that contained gardening tools and
there he was, gazing. He was looking at a new green metal
wheelbarrow with a red wheel and a rubber tyre and he had
even pulled it out. He pushed it back, and when he saw her
he said accusingly:

"This door has no lock. I do not like to see a door without
a lock. I will bring one this afternoon."

It was how she knew he had appointed himself.

"But who will do your taxi work?"

"My son will do that," he said.

From that moment he owned her and the house.

"There will be a lot of toil in this vineyard," she said to
him maliciously and wished she had not said it; but Evans's
eyes lost their vacancy again and quickened and sparkled.
He gave a shout of laughter.

"Oh boy, there will!" he said, admiring her. And he went
off. She walked from room to room opening windows, and
from an upper one she saw distantly the white sheet of the
Gospel tent through the fir trees. She could settle to nothing.

It was an ugly house of large mean rooms, the landings
dark, the stairs steep. The furniture might have come out of
old-fashioned hotels and had the helpless look of objects
too large, ill-met commercially, and too gregarious. After
her mother's death, her father had moved his things into his
sister's house. Taste had not been a strong point in the
family. The books, mainly sermons, were her grandfather's;
his son had lived on a hoard of engineering textbooks and

magazines. Her sister read chiefly the Bible and the rest of her time changed her clothes, having the notion that she might be going out.

What paralysed Miss Freshwater's niece was the emptiness of the place. She had expected to disturb ghosts if she opened a drawer. She had expected to remember herself. Instead, as she waited for Evans to come on the first day she had the sensation of being ignored. Nothing watched in the shadows, nothing blinked in the beams of sunlight slanting across the room. The room she had slept in meant nothing. To fit memories into it was a task so awkward and artificial that she gave up trying. Several times she went to the window, waiting for Evans to walk in at the gate and for the destruction to begin.

When he did come he seized the idea at once. All files marked "A.H.F."—that was her father—were "rubbish."

"Thorpe?" he said. "A.H.F., more A.H.F.! Burn it?" He was off with his first load to lay the foundation to the fire.

"And get this carpet up. We shall trip on it: it is torn," she said. He ripped the carpet off the stairs. He tossed the door mats, which were worn into holes, outside. By the barrow load out went the magazines. Every now and then some object took his eye—a leather strap, a bowl, a pipe rack—which he put into a little heap of other perquisites at the back door.

But to burn was his passion, to push the wheelbarrow his joy. He swaggered with it. He unloaded it carefully at the fire, not putting it down too near or roughly tipping it. He often tried one or two different grips on the handles before he started off. Once, she saw him stop in the middle of the lawn and turn it upside-down and look it over carefully and make the wheel spin. Something wrong? No, he lovingly wiped the wheel with a handful of grass, got an oil can from his pocket, and gave the wheel a squirt. Then he righted the wheelbarrow and came on with it round the house, singing in a low and satisfied voice. A hymn, it sounded like. And at the end of the day, when she took him a cup of tea and they stood chatting, his passion satisfied for the time being, he had a good look at her. His eye was on the brooch she was carelessly wearing to fasten her green overall. He came closer and put his hand to the brooch and lifted it.

"Those are pearls, I shouldn't wonder?" he said.

"Yes," she said. He stepped nimbly away, for he was as quick as a flea.

"It is beautiful," he said, considering the brooch and herself together. "You would not buy it for fifty pounds, nor even a hundred, I suppose. A present, I expect?" And before she could answer, he said gravely: "Half past five! I will lock the sheds. Are you sleeping here? My wife would go off her head, alone in the house. When I'm at the mission, she's insane!"

Evans stared at Miss Freshwater's niece, waiting for a response to his drama. She did not know what to do, so she laughed. Evans gave a shout of laughter too. It shook the close black curls of his hair and the scar on the side of his nose went white.

"I have the key," he said seriously and went off.

"Robert!" Miss Freshwater's niece opened the window and called again. "Can you come now? I can't get on."

Evans was on his way back to the house. He stamped quickly up the bare stairs.

The Wheelbarrow

"I'm in here," she called. "If you can get in!"

There was a heap of old brown paper knee high at the door. Some of the drawers of a chest had been taken out, others were half open; a wardrobe's doors were open wide. There were shoes, boxes, and clothes piled on the bed, which was stripped. She had a green scarf in a turban round her head, and none of her fair hair could be seen. Her face, with its strong bones and pale skin marked by dirty fingers, looked hard, humorous, and naked. Her strong lips were dry and pale with dust.

They understood each other. At first he had bossed her, but she had fought back on the second day and they were equals now. She spoke to him as if they were in a conspiracy together, deciding what should be "saved" and what should be "cast into the flames." She used those words purposely, as a dig of malice at him. She was taller than he. She couldn't get over the fact that he preached every night at the mission and she had fallen into the habit of tempting him by some movement of arm or body, when she caught him looking at her. Her aunt had used the word "inconvenient," when her niece was young, to describe the girl's weakness for dawdling about with gardeners, chauffeurs, errand boys. Miss Freshwater's niece had lost the sense of the "convenient" very early in life.

"I've started upstairs now," she said to Evans. "It's worse than downstairs. Look at it."

Evans came a step further into the room and slowly looked round, nodding his head.

She leaned a little forward, her hands together, eagerly waiting for him to laugh so that they could laugh together.

"She never threw away a scrap of paper. Not even paper bags. Look at this," she said.

He waded into the heap and peeped into a brown paper bag. It contained a bun, as hard as stone.

"Biscuits too," she said. "Wrapped up! Like a larder. They must have been here for years. In the top drawer."

Evans did not laugh.

"She feared starvation," he said: "old people are hungry. They are greedy. My grandmother nibbled like a little rat, all day. And in the night too. They wake up in the night and they are afraid. They eat for comfort. The mice did not get in, I hope," he said, going to look in the drawer.

"She was eighty-four," she said.

"My grandmother was ninety," he said. "My father's mother. She liked to hear a mouse. It was company, she said."

"I think my aunt must have been fond of moths," she said. "They came out in clouds from that wardrobe. Look at all those dresses. I can hardly bear to touch them."

She shook a couple of dresses in the wardrobe and then took them out. "There you are, did you see it? There goes one."

She held up an old-fashioned silk dress.

"Not worn for twenty years, you can see by the fashion. There!" She gave the dress a pull. "Did you hear? Perished. Rotten. They are all like that. You can't give them away. They'd fall off you."

She threw the dresses on the floor and he picked up one and he saw where moths had eaten it.

"It is wicked," he said. "All that money gone to waste."

83

The Wheelbarrow

"Where moth and dust doth corrupt," she mocked him, and took an armful of the clothes and threw them on the floor. "Why did she buy them if she did not want them? And all those hats we had to burn? You haven't seen anything yet. Look at this."

On the bed was lying a pile of enormous lace-up corsets. Evans considered them.

"The men had patience," he said.

"Oh, she was not married," she said.

He nodded.

"That is how all the property comes to you, I suppose," he said. There was a shrewd flash in his blue eyes and she knew he had been gazing at her all this time and not at the clothes; but even as she caught his look the dissembling, still, vacant light slid back into it.

"Shoes!" she said, with excitement. "Do you want any shoes?" A large number of shoes of all kinds, little worn or not worn at all, were rowed in pairs on the bed and some had been thrown into a box as well.

"Fifty-one pairs I counted," she said. "She never went out but she went on ordering them. There's a piece of paper in each pair. Have a look. Read it. What does it say?"

He took a piece of paper out of a shoe.

" 'Comfortable for the evening,' " he read out. He took another. " 'For wet weather.' Did it rain indoors?"

She took one and read out: " 'With my blue dress'! Can you imagine? 'Sound walking pair.' " She laughed, but he interrupted her.

"In Wales they lacked them," he said. "In the bad times they were going barefoot. My sisters shared a pair for dances."

"What shall I do with them?" she asked. "Someone could wear them."

"There are good times now. They have the money," he said, snubbing her. "They buy new."

"I mean—anyone," she said. "They are too big for me. I'll show you."

She sat down on a packing case and slipped her foot into a silver evening shoe.

"You can see, my feet are lost in them," she said.

"You have small feet," he said. "In Wales the men would be chasing you."

"After chapel, I've no doubt," she said. "Up the mountain—what was the name of it? You told me."

"It has the best view in Wales. But those who go up it never see it," he laughed. "Try this pair," he said, kneeling down and lifting her foot. "Ah no, I see. But look at those legs, boy!"

Miss Freshwater's niece got up.

"What size does your wife take?" she asked.

"I don't know," he said, very pleased with himself. "Where is this trunk you said we had to move?"

"Out in the landing cupboard. I'll show you. I can't move it."

She led the way to the landing and bent down to tug at it.

"You must not do that," he said, putting his hands on her waist and moving her out of the way. He heaved at the trunk and tipped it on end. She wanted it, she said, in the light, where she could see.

"Here on the chest," she said.

He lifted it up and planked it down on the chest.

"Phew!" he said. "You have a small waist for a married

woman. Soft. My wife is a giantess, she weighs thirteen stone. And yet, you're big, too, oh yes, you are. But you have light bones. With her, now, it is the bones that weigh. Shall we open it?"

She sat down on a chair and felt in her pocket for a mirror.

"Why didn't you tell me I looked such a sight?" she said, wiping her face. "Yes, open it."

The trunk was made of black leather; it was cracked, peeling, stained, and squashed by use. Dimly printed on it was her father's fading name in white, large letters. The trunk had been pitched and bumped and slithered out of ships' holds and trains, all over the world. Its lid, now out of the true, no longer met the lock and it was closed by a strap. It had lain ripening and decaying in attics and lofts for half a lifetime.

"What is in it?" she called, without looking from her mirror.

"Clothes," he said. "Books. A pair of skates. Did the old lady go skating?"

He pulled out a Chinese hat. There was a pigtail attached to it and he held it up.

"Ah," he called. "This is the job." He put the hat on his head and pulled out a mandarin coat.

Miss Freshwater's niece stared and then she flushed.

"Where did you get that?" she cried, jumping up, taking the hat from his head and snatching the coat. "They're mine! Where were they?"

She pushed him aside and pulled one or two things from the trunk.

"They're mine!" she accused him. "All mine."

86

She aged as she looked at him. A photograph fell to the floor as she lifted up a book. " 'To darling Laura,' " she read out. "Tennyson."

"Who is this?" he said, picking up the photograph.

She did not hear. She was pulling out a cold, sequined evening dress that shrank almost to nothing as she picked it up.

"Good God," she said and dropped it with horror. For under the dress was an album. "Where," she said, sharply possessive, "did you put the skates?" She opened the album. She looked at a road deep in snow leading to a hotel with eaves a yard wide. She had spent her honeymoon there.

"Kitzbühel," she said. "Oh, no!"

She looked fiercely at him to drive him away. The house, so anonymous, so absurd, so meaningless and ghostless, had suddenly got her. There was a choke of cold wonder in her throat.

She turned on him. "Can't you clear up all that paper in the room?" She did not want to be seen by him.

Evans went to the door of the bedroom and, after a glance inside, came back. He was not going to leave her. He picked up the book of poems, glanced at a page or two, and then dropped it back in the trunk.

"Everyone knows," he said scornfully, "that the Welsh are the founders of all the poetry of Europe."

She did not hear him. Her face had drained of waking light. She had entered blindly into a dream in which she could hardly drag herself along. She was looking painfully through the album, rocking her head slowly from side to side, her mouth opening a little and closing on the point of speech, a shoulder rising as if she had been hurt, and her

87

back moving and swaying as she felt the clasp of the past like hands on her. She was looking at ten forgotten years of her life, her own life, not her family's, and she did not laugh when she saw the skirts too long, the top-heavy hats hiding the eyes, her face too full and fat, her plainness so sullen, her prettiness too open-mouthed and loud, her look too grossly sly. In this one, sitting at the café table by the lake when she was nineteen, she looked masterful and at least forty. In this garden picture she was theatrically fancying herself as an ancient Greek in what looked like a nightgown! One of her big toes, she noticed, turned up comically in the sandal she was wearing. Here on a rock by the sea, in a bathing dress, she had got thin again—that was her marriage—and look at her hair! This picture of the girl on skis, sharp-faced, the eyes narrowed—who was that? Herself—yet how could she have looked like that! But she smiled a little at last at the people she had forgotten. This man with the crinkled fair hair, a German—how mad she had been about him. But what pierced her was that in each picture of herself she was just out of reach, flashing and yet dead; and that really it was the things that burned in the light of permanence—the chairs, the tables, the trees, the car outside the café, the motor launch on the lake. These blinked and glittered. They had lasted and were ageless, untouched by time, and she was not. She put the album back into the trunk and pulled out an old tweed coat and skirt. Under it was an exercise book with the word "Diary" written on it in a hand more weakly rounded than the hand she wrote today. Part of a letter fell out of the Diary, the second page it seemed, of a letter of her own. She read it.

". . . the job at any rate," she read. "For a whole week

he's forgotten his chest, his foot, his stomach. He's not dying any more!!! He conde (crossed out) congratulates himself and says it just shows how doctors are all fools. Inner self-confidence is what I need, he tells me!! It means giving up the flat and that's what I keep thinking—Oxford will be much more difficult for you and me. Women, he says, aren't happy unless they're sacrificing themselves. Darling, he doesn't know: it's the thought of You that keeps . . ."

She turned over the page. Nothing. She looked through the Diary. Nothing. She felt sick and then saw Evans had not gone and was watching her. She quickly put the letter back into the Diary.

"Ah," she said nervously. "I didn't know you were here. I'll show you something." She laughed unnaturally and opened the album until she found the most ludicrous and abashing picture in the book, one that would humiliate her entirely. "Here, look at this."

There was a see-saw in the foreground surrounded by raucously laughing people wearing paper hats and looking as though they had been dipped in glycerine: she was astride at the higher end of the see-saw, kicking her legs, and on the lower end was a fat young man in a pierrot costume. On her short, fuzzy, fair hair was a paper hat. She showed the picture to Evans and picked out the terrible sequin dress from the trunk.

"That's the dress!" she said, pointing to the picture. "I was engaged to him. Isn't it terrible?" And she dropped the dress back again. It felt cold and slippery, almost wet. "I didn't marry him."

Evans scowled.

"You were naked," he said with disgust.

"I remember now. I left it all here. I kept that dress for years. I'll have to go through it all." And she pulled down the lid.

"This photograph fell out," he said.

It was the picture of another young man.

"Is this your husband?" Evans asked, studying the man.

"My husband is dead," she said sharply. "That is a friend." And she threw the picture back into the trunk. She realized now that Evans had been holding her arm a long time. She stepped away from him abruptly. The care-less friendliness, the sense of conspiracy she had felt while they worked together, had gone. She drew away and said, in the hostile voice of unnecessary explanation:

"I mean," she said, "my husband died a few years ago. We were divorced. I mustn't waste any more time."

"My wife would not condescend to that," he said.

"She has no reason, I am sure," said Miss Freshwater's niece, severely, and returned to the bedroom.

"Now! We can't waste time like this. You'd better begin with what is on the bed. And when you've cleared it you can put the kettle on."

When Evans had gone downstairs with his load, she went to the landing and glared at the trunk. Her fists were clenched; she wished it was alive and that she could hit it. Glancing over the banisters to be sure she was alone, she opened it again, took out the photograph and the letter from her diary and put them in her handbag. She thought she was going to be sick or faint, for the past was drumming, like a train coming nearer and nearer, in her head.

"My God," she said. And when she saw her head in its turban and her face hardened by shock and grief in her

90

aunt's absurd dressing-table mirror, she exclaimed with real horror. She was crying. "What a mess," she said and pulled the scarf off her head. Her fair, thick hair hung round her face untidily. Not once, in all those photographs, had a face so wolfish with bitterness and without laughter looked back at her.

"I'm taking the tea out," Evans called from below.

"I'm just coming," she called back and hurriedly tried to arrange her hair and then, because she had cried a little, she put on her glasses. Evans gave a keen look at the change in her when she got downstairs and walked through the hall to the door.

He had put the tray on the grass near a yew hedge in the hot corner at the side of the house and was standing a few yards away drinking his tea. In the last two days he had never drunk his tea near her but had chatted from a distance.

In her glasses and with her hair girlishly brushed back, Miss Freshwater's niece looked cold, tall, and grand, like a headmistress.

"I hope we shan't get any more smoke here," she said. "Sit down. You look too restless."

She was very firm, nodding to the exact place on the lawn on which she required him to sit. Taken aback, Evans sat precisely in that place. She sat on the grass and poured herself a cup of tea.

"How many souls came to Jesus last night?" she asked in her lady-like voice. Evans got up and squatted cheerfully, but watchfully, on his heels.

"Seventeen," he said.

"That's not very good," she said. "Do you think you could save mine?"

"Oh, yes," he said keenly.

"You look like a frog," she said, mocking. He had told her miners always squat in this way after work. "It's too late," she went on. "Twenty years too late. Have you always been with the mission?"

"No," he said.

"What was it? Were you converted, did you see the light?" she mocked, like a teacher.

"I had a vision," he said seriously.

"A vision!" she laughed. She waved her hand. "What do you mean—you mean, you—well, where? Up in the sky or something?"

"No," he said. "It was down the mine."

"What happened?"

He put down his cup and he moved it away to give himself more room. He squatted there, she thought, not like a frog at all, but like an imp or a devil, very grave and carven-faced. She noticed now how wide his mouth was and how widely it opened and how far the lips drew back when he spoke in his declamatory voice. He stared a long time waiting for her to stop fidgeting. Then he began.

"I was a drunkard," he declaimed, relishing each syllable separately. "I was a liar. I was a hypocrite. I went with women. And married women, too!" His voice rose. "I was a fornicator. I was an adulterer. Always at the races, too, gambling: it was senseless. There was no sin the Devil did not lead me into; I was like a fool. I was the most note-worthy sinner in the valley; everyone spoke of it. But I did not know the Lord was lying in wait for me."

"Yes, but what happened?" she said.

He got to his feet and gazed down at her and she was compelled to look up at him.

"I will tell you," he said. "It was a miracle." He changed his manner, and after looking round the garden, he said in a hushing and secretive voice:

"There was a disaster in the mine," he said. "It was in June. I was twenty-three and I was down working and I was thinking of the sunlight and the hills and the evening. There was a young girl called Alys Davies, you know, two or three had been after her and I was thinking I would take her up the rock, that is a quiet place, only an old mountain ram would see you. . . ."

"You were in the mine," she said. "You are getting too excited about this Alys Jones. . . ."

"Davies," he said with a quick grin. "Don't worry about her. She is married now." He went back to his solemn voice.

"And suddenly," he said, "there was a fall, a terrible fall of rock like thunder and all the men shouting. It was at eleven in the morning when we stopped work for our tea. There were three men in there working with me and they had just gone off. I was trapped alone."

"Were you hurt?" she said anxiously.

"It was a miracle, not a stone touched me. I was in a little black cave. It was like a tomb. I was in that place alone for twelve hours. I could hear them working to get at me, but after the first fall there was a second and then I thought I was finished. I could hear nothing."

"What did you do? I would have gone out of my mind," she said. "Is that how you got the scar on your nose?"

"That was in a fight," he said, offhand. "Madness is a

93

terrible thing. I stared into the blackness and I tried to think
of one thing to stop my mind wandering but I could not at
first for the fear, it was chasing and jumping like a mad dog
in my head. I prayed, and the more I prayed, the more it
chased and jumped. And then, suddenly, it stopped. I saw in
my mind a picture. I saw the mantelpiece at home and on it
a photograph of our family—my father and mother, my
four sisters and my brother. And we had an aunt and uncle
just married; it was a wedding photograph. I could see it
clearly as if I had been in my home. They were standing
there looking at me and I kept looking at them and thinking
about them. I held on to them. I kept everything else out of
my mind; wherever I looked that picture was before my
eyes. It was like a vision. It saved me."

"I have heard people say they hear voices," said Miss
Freshwater's niece, kindly now.

"Oh, no! They were speechless," said Evans. "Not a
word! I spoke to them," he said. "Out loud. I promised God
in front of all my family that I would cleanse my soul when
I got out."

Evans stood blazing in his trance and then he picked up
his cup from the grass and took it to her.

"May I please have some more tea?" he said.

"Of course," she said. "Sit down."

He considered where he should sit and then put himself
beside her.

"When I saw you looking at your photographs," he said,
"I thought: 'She is down the mine.'"

"I have never been down a mine in my life. I don't know
why. We lived near one once when I was in the north," she
evaded.

94

"The mine of the past," he said. "The dark mine of the past."

"I can see why you are a preacher, Robert." She smiled. "It's funny how one cannot get one's family out of one's head. I could feel mine inside me for years—but not now."

She had entirely stopped mocking him.

"I can't say they ever saved me," she said. "I think they nearly ruined me. Look at that ugly house and all that rubbish. Did you ever see anything like their furniture? When I was a girl I used to think: 'Suppose I got to look like that sideboard!' And then money was all they ever talked about—and good and nice people, and nice people always had money. It was like that in those days; thank God that has gone. Perhaps it hasn't. I decided to get away from it and I got married. They ought to have stopped me—all I wanted was to get away—but they thought my husband had money, too. He just had debts and a bad stomach. When he spent all my money, he just got ill to punish me. . . . You don't know anything about life when you're young, and when you are old it's too late. . . ."

"That's a commonplace remark," she went on, putting her cup on the tray and reaching for his. "My mother used to make it." She picked up her scarf and began to tie it on her head, but as she was tying it Evans quickly reached for it and pulled it off. His hand held the nape of her neck gently.

"You are not old," he shouted, laughing and sparkling. "Your hair is golden, not a grey one in it, boy."

"Robert, give me that scarf. It is to keep out the dust," she said, blushing. She reached for the scarf and he caught her wrist.

95

The Wheelbarrow

"When I saw you standing at the station on Monday, I said: 'Now, there is a woman! Look at the way she stands, a golden woman, that is the first I have seen in this town, she must be a stranger,' " he said.

"You know all the others, I expect," she said with amusement.

"Oh, indeed, yes I do! All of them!" he said. "I would not look at them twice."

His other hand slipped from her neck to her waist.

"I can trust myself with them, but not with you," he said, lowering his voice and speaking down to her neck. "In an empty house," he whispered, nodding to the house, letting go of her hand and stroking her knee.

"I am far past that sort of thing," said Miss Freshwater's niece, choosing a lugubrious tone. She removed his arm from her waist. And she stood up, adroitly picking up the tray, and from behind that defence, she looked round the garden. Evans sprang up, but instead of coming near her, he jumped a few yards away and squatted on his heels, grinning at her confidently.

"You look like the Devil," she said.

He had placed himself between her and the way to the house.

"It is quiet in the garden, too," he said with a wink. And then she saw the wheelbarrow, which he had left near the fire.

"That barrow ought to go well in the sale," she said. "It is almost new. How much do you think it will fetch?"

Evans stood up at once and his grin went. An evasive light, almost the light of tears, came into his hot blue eyes and he stared at her with an alarm that drove everything else out of his head.

"They'll put it with the tools, you will not get much for it."

"I think every man in the town will be after it," she said, with malice.

"What price did you want for it?" he said, uncertain of her.

"I don't know what they cost," she said carelessly and walked past him very slowly back to the house, maddening him by her walk. He followed her quickly, and when she turned, still carrying the tray, to face him in the doorway, she caught his agitation.

"I will take the tray to the kitchen," he said politely.

"No," she said, "I will do that. I want you to go upstairs and fetch down all those shoes. And the trunk. It can all go."

And she turned and walked through the house to the kitchen. He hesitated for a long time; at last she heard him go upstairs and she pottered in the kitchen, where the china and pans were stacked on the table, waiting for him to come down. He was a very long time. He came down with the empty trunk.

"It can all go. Burn it all. It's no good to anyone, damp and rotten. I've put aside what I want," she said.

He looked at her sullenly. He was startled by her manner and by the vehemence of her face, for she had put on the scarf and her face looked strong-boned, naked, and ruthless. She was startled herself.

His sullenness went; he returned to his old excitement and

97

hurried the barrow to the fire and she stood at the door impatiently waiting for the blaze. When he saw her waiting he came back.

"There it goes," he said with admiration.

The reflection of the flame danced in points of light in her eyes; her mouth was set, hard and bitter. Presently the flame dropped and greenish smoke came out thickly.

"Ah!" she gasped. Her body relaxed and she smiled at Evans, tempting him again.

"I've been thinking about the barrow," she said. "When we've finished up here, I'll make you a present of it. I would like to give it to you, if you have a use for it?"

She could see the struggle going on inside him as he boldly looked at her; and she saw his boldness pass into a small shrug of independent pride and the pride into pretence and dissembling.

"I don't know," he said, "that I have a use—well, I'll take it off you. I'll put the shoes in it, it will save bringing the car." He could not repress his eagerness any longer. "I'll put the shoes into it this evening. Thank you." He paused. "Thank you, ma'am," he said.

It was the first time he had called her "ma'am." The word was like a blow. The affair was over. It was, she realized, a dismissal.

An hour later she heard him rumbling the barrow down the path to the gate. The next day he did not come. He had finished with her. He sent his son up for his money.

It took Miss Freshwater's niece two more days to finish her work at the house. The heavy jobs had been done, except for putting the drawers back into the chests. She could have done with Evans's help there, and for the sweeping, which made her hot, but she was glad to be alone because she got on more quickly with the work. She hummed and even sang as she worked, feeling light and astonishingly happy. Once or twice, when she saw the white sheet of the mission tent distantly through the trees, she smiled.

"He got what he wanted! And I'm evidently not as old as I look."

The last hours buzzed by and she spun out the time, reluctant to go. She dawdled, locking the sheds, the windows and doors, until there was nothing more to keep her. She brought down a light suitcase in which she had put the few things she wanted to take away and she sat in the dining room, now as bare as an office, to go through her money. After the destruction she was having a fit of economy and it had occurred to her that instead of taking a taxi to the station, she could walk down to the bus stop on the Green. She knew that the happiness she felt was not ebbing, but had changed to a feeling she had not had for many years—the feeling of expectancy—and as this settled in her, she put her money and her papers back into her bag. There was a last grain of rubbish here: with scarcely a glance at them, she tore up the photograph and the unfinished letter she had found in the trunk.

"I owe Evans a lot," she thought.

Nothing retained her now.

She picked up her case. She left the house and walked down the road in the strong shade of the firs and the broad shade of the oak trees, whose leaves hardened with populous contentment in the long evening light. When she got to the open Green, children were playing round the Gospel tent and, in two's and three's, people were walking from the houses across the grass towards it. She had twenty minutes to wait until her bus arrived. She heard the sound of singing coming from the tent. She wondered if Evans would be there.

"I might give him the pleasure of seeing what he missed," she thought.

She strolled across to the tent.

A youth who had watered his hair and given it a twirl with a comb was standing in his best clothes at the entrance to the tent.

"Come to Jesu! Come to Jesu!" he said to her as she peeped inside.

"I'm just looking for someone," she said politely.

The singing had stopped when she looked in, but the worshippers were still standing. They were packed in the white light of the tent and the hot smell of grass and somewhere at the far end, invisible, a man was shouting like a cheap jack selling something at an auction. He stopped suddenly and a high, powerful, country voice whined out alone: "Ow in the vale . . ." and the congregation joined in for another long verse.

"Is Mr. Evans here tonight?" she asked the youth.

"Yes," he said. "He's witnessing every night."

"Where is he? I don't see him."

The verse came to an end and once more a voice began talking at the other end of the tent. It was a woman's voice, high and incomprehensible and sharp. The hymn began again and then spluttered into an explosive roar that swept across the Green.

"They've fixed it. The loud speaker!" the youth exclaimed. Miss Freshwater's niece stepped back. The noises thumped. Sadly, she looked at her watch and began to walk back to the bus stop. When she was about ten yards from the tent, the loud speaker gave a high whistle and then, as if God had cleared his throat, spoke out with a gross and miraculous clearness.

"Friends," it said, sweeping right across the Green until it struck the furthest houses and the trees. "My friends . . ."

The word seemed to grind her and everyone else to nothing, to mill them all into the common dust.

"When I came to this place," it bellowed, "the serpent . . ." (an explosion of noise followed, but the voice cleared again) . . . heart. No bigger than a speck it was at first, as tiny as a speck of coal grit in your eye . . ."

Miss Freshwater's niece stopped. Was it Evans's voice? A motor coach went by on the road and drowned the next words, and then she heard, spreading into an absurd public roar:

"I was a liar. I was an adulterer. Oh my friends, I was a slave of the strange woman the Bible tells about, the whore of Babylon, in her palace where moth and dust . . ." Detonations again.

But it was Evans's voice. She waited and the enormously magnified voice burst through.

"And then by the great mercy of the Lord I heard a voice cry out: 'Robert Evans, what are you doing, boy? Come out of it. . . .' " But the voice exploded into meaningless concussions, suddenly resuming:

The Wheelbarrow

". . . and burned the adulteress in the everlasting fire, my friends—and all her property."

The hymn started up again.

"Well, not quite all, Robert," said Miss Freshwater's niece pleasantly aloud, and a child eating an ice cream near her watched her walk across the grass to the bus stop.

The Fall

It was the evening of the annual dinner. More than two hundred accountants were at that hour changing into evening clothes, in the flats, villas, and hotel rooms of a large, wet, Midland city. At the Royal was Charles Peacock, slender in his shirt, balancing on one leg and gazing with frowns of affection in the wardrobe mirror at the other leg as he pulled his trouser on; and then with a smile of farewell as the second went in. Buttoned up, relieved of nakedness, he visited other mirrors—the one at the dressing table, the two in the bathroom, assembling the scattered aspects of the unsettled being called Peacock "doing," as he was apt to say, "not so badly" in this city that smelled of coal and where thirty-eight years ago he had been born. When he left his room there were mirrors in the hotel lift and down below in the foyer and outside in the street. Certain shop windows were favourable and assuring. The love affair was taken up again at the Assembly rooms by the mirrors in the tiled corridor leading towards the bullocky noise of two hundred-odd chartered accountants in black ties, taking their drinks under the chandeliers that seemed to weep above their heads.

103

The Fall

Crowds or occasions frightened Peacock. They engaged him, at first sight, in the fundamental battle of his life: the struggle against nakedness, the panic of grabbing for clothes and becoming someone. An acquaintance in a Scottish firm was standing near the door of the packed room as Peacock went in.

"Hullo, laddie," Peacock said, fitting himself out with a Scottish accent, as he went into the crowded, chocolate-coloured buffet.

"What's to do?" he said, passing on to a Yorkshireman.

"Are you well now?" he said, in his Irish voice. And, gaining confidence, "Whatcha cock!" to a man up from London, until he was shaking hands in the crowd with the President himself, who was leaning on a stick and had his foot in plaster.

"I hope this is not serious, sir," said Peacock in his best southern English, nodding at the foot.

"Bloody serious," said the President, sticking out his peppery beard. "I caught my foot in a grating. Some damn fools here think I've got gout."

No one who saw Peacock in his office, in Board rooms, on committees, at meetings, knew the exhausting number of rough sketches that had to be made before the naked Peacock could become Peacock dressed for his part. Now, having spoken to several human beings, the fragments called Peacock closed up. And he had one more trick up his sleeve if he panicked again: he could drop into music-hall Negro.

Peacock got a drink at the buffet table and pushed his way to a solitary island of carpet two feet square, in the guffawing corral. He was looking at the back of the President's neck. Almost at once the President, on the crest of a successful joke he had told, turned round with appetite.

"Hah!" he shouted. "Hah! Here's friend Peacock again."

"Why 'again'?" thought Peacock.

The President looked Peacock over.

"I saw your brother this afternoon," shouted the President. The President's injured foot could be said to have made his voice sound like a hilarious smash. Peacock's drink jumped and splashed his hand. The President winked at his friends.

"Hah!" said the President. "That gave our friend Peacock a scare!"

"At the Odeon," explained a kinder man.

"Is Shelmerdine Peacock your brother? The actor?" another said, astonished, looking at Peacock from head to foot.

"Shelmerdine Peacock was born and bred in this city," said the President fervently.

"I saw him in *Waste*," someone said. And others recalled him in *The Gun Runner* and *Doctor Zut*.

Four or five men stood gazing at Peacock with admiration, waiting for him to speak.

"Where is he now?" said the President, stepping forward, beard first. "In Hollywood? Have you seen him lately?"

They all moved forward to hear about the famous man.

Peacock looked to the right—he wanted to do this properly—but there was no mirror in that direction; he looked to the left, but there was no mirror there. He lowered his head gravely and then looked up shaking his head sorrowfully. He brought out the old reliable Negro voice.

The Fall

"The last time I saw l'il ole brudder Shel," he said, "he was being thrown out of the Orchid Room. He was calling the waiters 'goatherds.' "

Peacock looked up at them all and stood, collected, assembled, whole at last, among their shouts of laughter. One man who did not laugh and who asked what the Orchid Room was, was put in his place. And in a moment a voice bawled from the door: "Gentlemen. Dinner is served." The crowd moved through two anterooms into the great hall, where, from their portraits on the wall, mayors, presidents, and justices looked down with the complacent rosiness of those who have dined and died. It was gratifying to Peacock that the President rested his arm on his shoulder for a few steps as they went into the hall.

Shel often cropped up in Peacock's life, especially in clubs and at dinners. It was pleasing. There was always praise; there were always questions. He had seen the posters about Shel's film during the week on his way to his office. They pleased, but they also troubled. Peacock stood at his place at table in the great hall and paused to look around, in case there was one more glance of vicarious fame to be collected. He was enjoying one of those pauses of self-possession in which, for a few seconds, he could feel the sensations Shel must feel when he stepped before the curtain to receive the applause of some great audience in London or New York. Then Peacock sat down. More than two hundred soup spoons scraped.

"Sherry, sir," said the waiter.

Peacock sipped.

He meant no harm to Shel, of course. But in a city like this, with Shel appearing in a big picture, with his name fifteen feet long on the hoardings, talked about by girls in offices, the universal instinct of family disparagement was naturally tickled into life. The President might laugh and the crowd admire, but it was not always agreeable for the family to have Shel roaming loose—and often very loose—in the world. One had to assert the modesty, the anonymity of the ordinary assiduous Peacocks. One way of doing this was to add a touch or two to famous scandals: to enlarge the drunken scrimmages and add to the divorces and the breaches of contract, increase the overdoses taken by flighty girls. One was entitled to a little rake-off—an accountant's charges—from the fame that so often annoyed. One was entitled, above all, because one loved Shel.

"Hock, sir?" said the waiter.

Peacock drank. Yes, he loved Shel. Peacock put down his glass, and the man opposite him spoke across the table, a man with an amused mouth, who turned his sallow face sideways so that one had the impression of being enquired into under a loose lock of black hair by one sharp, serious eye only.

"An actor's life is a struggle," the man said. Peacock recognized him: it was the man who had not laughed at his story and who had asked what the Orchid Room was, in a voice that had a sad and puncturing feeling for information sought for its own sake.

Peacock knew this kind of admirer of Shel's and feared him. They were not content to admire, they wanted to advance into intimacy, and collect facts on behalf of some general view of life's mysteriousness. As an accountant Peacock rejected mystery.

"I don't think l'il ole brudder Shel has struggled much,"

said Peacock, wagging his head from side to side carelessly.

"I mean he has to dedicate himself," said the man.

Peacock looked back mistrustfully.

"I remember some interview he gave about his school days—in this city," said the man. "It interested me. I do the books for the Hippodrome."

Peacock stopped wagging his head from side to side. He was alert. What Shel had said about his early life had been damned tactless.

"Shel had a good time," said Peacock sharply. "He always got his own way."

Peacock put on his face of stone. He dared the man to say out loud, in that company, three simple English words. He dared him. The man smiled and did not say them.

"Volnay, sir," said the waiter as the pheasant was brought. Peacock drank.

"Fried Fish Shop," Peacock said to himself as he drank. Those were the words. "Shel could have kept his mouth shut about that. I'm not a snob, but why mention it? Why, after they were all doing well, bring ridicule upon the family? Why not say, simply: 'Shop'? Why not say, if he had to: 'Fishmonger'? Why mention 'Frying'? Why add: '*Bankrupt* Fried Fish Shop'?"

It was swinish, disloyal, ungrateful. Bankrupt—all right; but some of that money, Peacock said, hectoring the pheasant on his plate, paid for Shel's years at the Dramatic School. It was unforgivable.

Peacock looked across at the man opposite, but the man had turned to talk to a neighbour. Peacock finished his glass and chatted with the man sitting to his right, but he felt like telling the whole table a few facts about dedication.

"Dedication," he would have said. "Let us take a look at the figures. An example of Shel's dedication in those Fried Fish Shop days he is so fond of remembering to make fools of us. Saturday afternoon. Father asleep in the back room. Shel says: 'Come down the High Street with me, Tom. I want to get a record.' Classical, of course. Usual swindle. If we get into the shop he won't have the money and will try and borrow from me. 'No,' I say. 'I haven't got any money.' 'Well, let's get out of this stink of lard and fish.' He wears me down. He wore us all down, the whole family. He would be sixteen, two years older than me. And so we go out and at once I know there is going to be trouble. 'I saw the Devil in Cramer's,' he says. We go down the High Street to Cramer's—it's a music shop—and he goes up to the girl to ask if they sell bicycle pumps or rubber heels. When the girl says 'No,' he makes a terrible face at her and shouts out 'Bah.' At Hook's, the stationer's, he stands at the door and calls to the girl at the cash desk: 'You've got the Devil in here. I've reported it,' and slams the door. We go on to Bond's, the grocer's, and he pretends to be sick when he sees the bacon. Goes out. 'Rehearsing,' he says. The Bonds are friends of Father's. There is a row. Shel swears he was never anywhere near the place and goes back the following Saturday and falls flat on the floor in front of the Bond daughter, groaning: 'I've been poisoned. I'm dying. Water! Water! Falls flat on his back . . .' "

"Caught his foot in a grating, he told me, and fell," the man opposite was saying. "Isn't that what he told you, Peacock?"

Peacock's imaginary speech came suddenly to an end. The man was smiling as if he had heard every word.

"Who?" said Peacock.

"The President," said the man. "My friend, Mr. McAlister, is asking me what happened to the President. Did he fall in the street?"

Peacock collected himself quickly and to hide his nakedness became Scottish.

"Ay, mon." He nodded across the table. "A wee bit of a tumble in the street."

Peacock took up his glass and drank.

"He's a heavy man to fall," said the man called McAlister.

"He carries a lot of weight," said his neighbour. Peacock eyed him. The impression was growing that this man knew too much, too quietly. It struck him that the man was one of those who ask what they know already, a deeply unbelieving man. They have to be crushed.

"Weight makes no difference," said Peacock firmly.

"It's weight and distance," said the Scotsman. "Look at children."

Peacock felt a smile coming over his body from the feet upwards.

"Weight and distance make no difference," Peacock repeated.

"How can you say that?"

An enormous voice, hanging brutally on the air like a sergeant's, suddenly shouted in the hall. It was odd to see the men in the portraits on the wall still sitting down after the voice sounded. It was the voice of the toastmaster.

"Gen–tle–men!" it shouted. "I ask you. To rise to. The toast of Her. Maj–es–ty. The Queen."

Two hundred or more accountants pushed back their chairs and stood up.

"The Queen," they growled. And one or two, Peacock among them, fervently added: "God bless her," and drained his glass.

Two hundred or more accountants sat down. It was the moment Peacock loved. And he loved the Queen.

"Port or brandy, sir?" the waiter asked.

"Brandy," said Peacock.

"You were saying that weight and distance make no difference. How do you make that out?" the sidelong man opposite said in a sympathetic and curious voice that came softly and lazily out.

Peacock felt the brandy burn. The question floated by, answerable if seized as it went and yet, suddenly, unanswerable for the moment. Peacock stared at the question keenly as if it were a fly that he was waiting to swat when it came round again. Ah, there it came. Now! But no, it had gone by once more. It was answerable. He knew the answer. Peacock smiled, loosely biding his time. He felt the flame of authority, of absolute knowledge burn in him.

There was a hammering at the President's table, there was hand-clapping. The President was on his feet and his beard had begun to move up and down.

"I'll tell you later," said Peacock curtly across the table. The interest went out of the man's eye.

"Once more," the President's beard was saying, and it seemed sometimes that he had two beards. "Honour," said one beard; "privilege," said the other; "old friends," said both beards together. "Speeches . . . brief . . . reminded of story . . . shortest marriage service in the world . . . Tennessee . . ."

"Hah! Hah! Hah!" shouted a pack of wolves, hyenas, hounds in dinner jackets.

Peacock looked across at the unbeliever who sat opposite. The interest in weight and distance had died away in his face.

"Englishman . . . Irishman . . . Scotsman . . . train . . . Englishman said . . . Scotsman said . . . Och, says Paddy . . ."

"Hah! Hah! Hah!" from the pack.

Over the carnations in the silver-plated vases on the table, over the heads of the diners, the cigar smoke was rising sweetly and the first-level indigo shafts of it were tipping across the middle air and turning the portraits of the past masters into day-dreams. Peacock gazed at it. Then a bell rang in his ear, so loudly that he looked shyly to see if anyone else had heard it. The voice of Shel was on some line of his memory, a voice richer, more insinuating than the toastmaster's or the President's, a voice utterly flooring.

"Abel?" Shel was saying. "Is that you, Abel? This is Cain speaking. How's the smoke? Is it still going up straight to heaven? Not blowing about all over the place? . . ."

The man opposite caught Peacock's eye for a second, as if he too had heard the voice, and then turned his head away. And, just at the very moment when once more Peacock could have answered that question about the effect of weight and distance, the man opposite stood up; all the accountants stood up. Peacock was the last. There was another toast to drink. And immediately there was more hammering and another speaker. Peacock's opportunity was lost. The man opposite had moved his chair back from the table and was sitting sideways to the table, listening, his interest in Peacock gone for good.

Peacock became lonely. Sulkily he played with matchsticks and arranged them in patterns on the tablecloth. There was a point at annual dinners when he always did this. It was at that point when one saw the function had become fixed by a flash photograph in the gloss of celebration and when everyone looked sickly and old. Eyes became hollow, temples sank, teeth loosened. Shortly the diners would be carried out in coffins. One waited restlessly for the thing to be over. Ten years of life went by and then, it seemed, there were no more speeches. There was some business talk in groups; then two's and three's left the table. Others filed off into a large chamber next door. Peacock's neighbours got up. He, who feared occasions, feared even more their dissolution. It was like that frightening ten minutes in a theatre when the audience slowly moves out, leaving a hollow stage and row after row, always increasing, of empty seats behind them. In a panic Peacock got up. He was losing all acquaintance. He had even let the man opposite slip away, for that man was walking down the hall with some friends. Peacock hurried down his side of the long table to meet them at the bottom, and when he got there he turned and barred their way.

"What we were talking about," he said. "It's an art. Simply a matter of letting the breath go, relaxing the muscles. Any actor can do it. It's the first thing they learn."

"I'm out of my depth," said the Scotsman.

"Falling," said Peacock. "The stage fall." He looked at

them with dignity, then he let the expression die on his face. He fell quietly full length to the floor. Before they could speak he was up on his feet.

"My brother weighs two hundred and twenty pounds," he said with condescension to the man opposite. "The ordinary person falls and breaks an arm or a foot because he doesn't know. It's an art."

His eyes conveyed that if the Peacocks had kept a Fried Fish Shop years ago, they had an art.

"Simple," said Peacock. And down he went, thump, on the carpet again, and lying at their feet he said:

"Painless. Nothing broken. Not a bruise. I said 'an art.' Really one might call it a science. Do you see how I'm lying?"

"What's happened to Peacock?" said two or three men joining the group.

"He's showing us the stage fall."

"Nothing," said Peacock, getting up and brushing his coat sleeve and smoothing back his hair. "It is just a stage trick."

"I wouldn't do it," said a large man, patting his stomach.

"I've just been telling them—weight is nothing. Look." Peacock fell down and got up at once.

"You turn. You crumple. You can go flat on your back. I mean, that is what it looks like," he said.

And Peacock fell.

"Shel and I used to practise it in the bedroom. Father thought the ceiling was coming down," he said.

"Good God, has Peacock passed out?" A group standing by the fireplace in the hall called across. Peacock got up and, brushing his jacket again, walked up to them. The group he had left watched him. There was a thump.

"He's done it again," the man opposite said.

"Once more. There he goes. Look, he's going to show the President. He's going after him. No, he's missed him. The old boy has slipped out of the door."

Peacock was staring with annoyance at the door. He looked at other groups of two's and three's.

"Who was the casualty over there?" someone said to him as he walked past.

Peacock went over to them and explained.

"Like judo," said a man.

"No!" said Peacock indignantly, even grandly. And in Shel's manner. Anyone who had seen Shelmerdine Peacock affronted knew what he looked like. That large white face trod on you. "Nothing to do with judo. This is the theatre. . . ."

"Shelmerdine Peacock's brother," a man whispered to a friend.

"Is that so?"

"It's in the blood," someone said.

To the man who had said "judo," Peacock said: "No throwing, no wrestling, no somersaulting or fancy tricks. That is not theatre. Just . . . simply . . ." said Peacock. And crumpling, as Shel might have done in *Macbeth* or *Hamlet,* or like some gangster shot in the stomach, Peacock once more let his body go down with the cynicism of the skilful corpse. This time he did not get up at once. He looked up at their knees, their waists, at their goggling faces, saw under their double chins and under their hairy

eyebrows. He grinned at their absurdity. He saw that he
held them. They were obliged to look at him. Shel must
always have had this sensation of hundreds of astonished
eyes watching him lie, waiting for him to move. Their gaze
would never leave the body. He never felt less at a loss,
never felt more completely himself. Even the air was better
at carpet level; it was certainly cooler and he was glad of
that. Then he saw two pairs of feet advancing from another
group. He saw two faces peep over the shoulders of the
others, and heard one of them say:

"It's Peacock—still at it."

He saw the two pairs of boots and trousers go off. Peacock got to his feet at once and resentfully stared after them.
He knew something, as they went, that Shel must have
known: the desperation, the contempt for the audience that
is thinning out. He was still brushing his sleeve and trousers
legs when he saw everyone moving away out of the hall.
Peacock moved after them into the chamber.

A voice spoke behind him. It was the quiet, intimate voice
of the man with the loose lock of black hair who had sat
opposite him.

"You need a drink," the man said.

They were standing in the chamber, where the buffet
table was. The man had gone into the chamber and, clearly,
he had waited for Peacock. A question was going round as
fast as a catherine wheel in Peacock's head and there was no
need to ask it: it must be so blindingly obvious. He looked
for someone to put it to, on the quiet, but there were only
three men at the buffet table with their backs turned to him.
Why (the question ran) at the end of a bloody good dinner

is one always left with some awful drunk, a man you've never liked—an unbeliever?

Peacock mopped his face. The unbeliever was having a short, disgusting laugh with the men at the bar and now was coming back with a glass of whisky.

"Sit down. You must be tired," said the unbeliever.

They sat down. The man spoke of the dinner and the speeches. Peacock did not listen. He had just noticed a door leading into a small anteroom and he was wondering how he could get into it.

"There was one thing I don't quite get," the man said: "perhaps it was the quickness of the hand deceiving the eye. I should say 'feet.' What I mean is—do you first take a step, I mean like in dancing? I mean is the art of falling really a paradox—I mean the art of keeping your balance all the time?"

The word "paradox" sounded offensive to Peacock.

The man looked too damn clever, in Peacock's opinion, and didn't sit still. Wearily Peacock got up.

"Hold my drink," he said. "You are standing like this, or facing sideways—on a level floor, of course. On a slope like this . . ."

The man nodded.

"I mean—well, now, watch carefully. Are you watching?"

"Yes," said the man.

"Look at my feet," said Peacock.

"No," said the man, hastily, putting out a free hand and catching Peacock by the arm. "I see what you mean. I was just interested in the theory."

117

The Fall

Peacock halted. He was offended. He shook the man's arm off.

"Nothing theoretical about it," he said and, shaking his sleeves, added: "No paradox."

"No," said the man, standing up and grabbing Peacock so that he could not fall. "I've got the idea." He looked at his watch. "Which way are you going? Can I give you a lift?"

Peacock was greatly offended. To be turned down! He nodded to the door of the anteroom. "Thanks," he said. "The President's waiting for me."

"The President's gone," said the man. "Oh well, good night." And he went away. Peacock watched him go. Even the men at the bar had gone. He was alone.

"But thanks," he called after him. "Thanks."

Cautiously Peacock sketched a course into the anteroom. It was a small, high room, quite empty and yet, one would have said, packed with voices, chattering, laughing, and mixed with music along the pannelled walls, but chiefly coming from behind the heavy green velvet curtains that were drawn across the window at one end. There were no mirrors, but Peacock had no need of them. The effect was ornate—gilded pillars at the corners, a small chandelier rising and falling gracefully from a carven ceiling. On the wall hung what, at first, sight, seemed to be two large oil paintings of queens of England, but, on going closer, Peacock saw there was only one oil painting—of Queen Victoria. Peacock considered it. The opportunity was enormous. Loyally, his face went blank. He swayed, loyally fell, and loyally got to his feet. The Queen might or might not have clapped her little hands. So encouraged, he fell again and got up. She was still sitting there.

"Shel," said Peacock, aloud to the Queen, "has often acted before Royalty. He's in Hollywood now, having left me to settle all his tax affairs. Hundreds of documents. All lies, of course. And there is this case for alimony going on. He's had four wives," he said to Queen Victoria. "That's the side of theatre life I couldn't stand, even when we were boys. I could see it coming. But—watch me," he said.

And delightfully he crumpled, the perfect backwards spin. Leaning up on his elbow from where he was lying, he waited for her to speak.

She did not speak, but two or three other queens joined her, all crowding and gossiping together, as Peacock got up. The Royal box! It was full. Cars hooting outside the window behind the velvet curtains had the effect of an orchestra and then, inevitably, those heavy green curtains were drawn up. A dark, packed, and restless auditorium opened itself to him. There was dense applause.

Peacock stepped forward in awe and wholeness. Not to fall, not to fall, this time, he murmured. To bow. One must bow and bow and bow and not fall, to the applause. He set out. It was a strangely long up-hill journey towards the footlights, and not until he got there did it occur to him that he did not know how to bow. Shel had never taught him. Indeed, at the first attempt the floor came up and hit him in the face.

The Necklace

Just checking up on a necklace your wife brought in this afternoon," the older of the two detectives said to me when we got to the police station. He was sucking a peppermint and was short of breath. The younger one kept his hands in his raincoat pockets and didn't say a word, and neither did I. We went into an inner room and sat down. I was afraid of having a smile too big for my face; my mouth was watering. All the time, I could feel the words swelling up in me: "We only did our duty." If you find something in the street, you take it to the police. Of course, if it's valuable you may get a reward. But not necessarily. Anyway, you don't do it for the reward. But all that week I'd kept my eyes open for a notice saying "Reward." Then the young detective pulled the necklace out of his pocket and put it on the table. "Do you recognize this, Mr. Drayton?" he asked.

I recognized it at once. "That's it," I said. "I found it Saturday."

Exactly where, they asked, and what time? I told them.

"Do you know who it belongs to?" they asked.

"If I'd known, I would have taken it to them," I said. "I

wouldn't have brought it here." It was a silly question, and the next ones were silly, too.

"It doesn't belong to you?" the young one asked.

"Or your wife?" asked the older one.

"Definitely not," I said. "I found it in the street, I told you."

"Do you know a Mrs. Faber?" the young one asked.

"No," I said. "What's she got to do with it?"

"You're a window cleaner, aren't you?" asked the older one. "She lives at Seventeen Launceston Road. Do you do a job there?"

"No," I said. "I do twenty-four, fifty-one, and the flats at the end. What's the idea?"

"And you say you found it at the corner of Alston Street and the Promenade on Saturday?"

"That's it. I just told you," I said.

"Just checking up. We have to check up on all lost property," said the older one. And the young one must have had a nod from him, because he got up and left the room. I looked up at the dark-green, glossy walls and the frosted window, and then I heard Nell's voice and her heels on the floor outside in the passage.

I sat there trying to remember everything as her voice came nearer, but there wasn't time. The one thing I could think of was Saturday, January 11: all that rain, and the football match; we beat Hopley Rangers, 3–0. Even when I have been going over it since, my mind gets stuck there. Saturdays, in the season, I used to pack up the job early and go home to my dinner, and when Plushy came round —my mate, Plushy Edwards—we would go off. We'd both been playing for the Rovers a couple of years. Nell some-

The Necklace

times came, too, but she didn't take to Plushy much. Come to that, she must have hated him. It went back to the time when she first met me, and Plushy told her I was a married man with two children and not to break up a happy home. Plushy was always having a lark like that with her. "I don't like men who tell lies," Nell said. It worried her when people made jokes. She really believed them.

But as I say: Saturday, football, I am coming round Alston Street off the Promenade, on my way home, and there it is: a necklace with three strands of big pearls, lying in the gutter. I looked up and down the Promenade. The weather was squally; the rain had browned the pebbles on the beach and had softened the sishing of the sea. The only moving things in sight were the back of a bus that had passed and two or three children running out of the rain a long way off, and the sea gulls. I looked down at the gutter again. It surprised me the necklace was still there. I propped my bike against a lamp and went back and picked the thing up. The pearls were hard and cold, like rice, but wet. I wiped the dirt off them and looked up at the windows of the houses. If there had been someone looking out, I would have shouted: "Anyone lost anything?" There was no one. I don't mind admitting that seeing a thing like this upset me. In this job, you see money, watches, and rings left about on desks and dressing tables the whole time. It doesn't worry me, but it annoys me. People miss something, and the next thing they're saying: "It's the window cleaner." I put the necklace into my pocket and I got on my bike. But the rain started coming down hard now, and I thought: "This means no blooming football." Plushy was waiting at my house already, just as fed-up as I was about the weather. The necklace went out of my head.

"Here, lay off. I'm a bachelor," said Plushy when I kissed my wife.

"You're late," she said to me. She always said that. "You two aren't playing football in this, are you? You're wet."

"Yes, look at his hair. That German crop never suited him, did it, Nell?" said Plushy, starting his usual larks, and pretending to dribble a ball round our kitchen as he spoke. "And where have you been? Hill Street? That blonde at twenty-seven, I bet. Look at his face! No, he's not been near Hill Street—oh, no! Dear, oh dear, oh dear!"

"I did Launceston Road this morning," I said.

"I thought you were going up the avenue," my wife said. Her grey eyes looked empty and truthful.

"I did the avenue yesterday," I said.

We had been married two years, and this was her way of loving me—knowing everything I did. Now and then she overloved me by getting it wrong. When I was out on the job, I would have the idea she was with me, because I was always thinking of her. So when she said she thought I was up the avenue, I felt confused, as if she had been up there and I hadn't spotted her; or as if I ought to say I had been up the avenue, so that she wouldn't have missed me. See what I mean? Sounds silly. I was so soppy about her that I didn't know which was me and which was Nell.

"Coming to the game, Nell?" Plushy asked her, and when she said she had something better to do than stand in the mud and the rain, Plushy left me alone and started on her. "What's she up to, Jim?" he asked me.

123

The Necklace

"Ironing," she said. "I'm sorry for the poor girl who has to do yours. Have you found her?"

"There'll be no tears at Plushy's wedding," I said. It was one of my mother's sayings.

"It'll be more like a court case," Nell said seriously.

"Jim, she means it," said Plushy.

I changed my clothes, and at two o'clock Plushy and I went off.

I took up window-cleaning when I came out of the army. Plushy persuaded me into it. The money was good. He said he'd heard women all over the country crying out loud in every street to get their windows cleaned. "Just count the windows in this town," he said to me. "More windows than people. Every window a ruddy SOS. Someone's got to do them." But Plushy got fed-up with it after a year. The women got him down. "They're screaming all day for you," he said. "You turn up and it's the wrong time. Women at you all day long—following you round the house, watching to see you don't mark their curtains or spoil their carpets, calling upstairs to someone to lock the drawers: 'It's the window cleaner.' Like they'd got the burglars in." Plushy went off to work in a factory, but I liked being on my own. I stayed on, took over some of his customers. That is how I met Nell.

"Bad luck to see the new moon through glass," Plushy said when I told him about meeting her, and she did look sort of moony. She was in the back bedroom of a house in the avenue, fixing her earrings and doing up her face, when I came up the ladder outside. She had reddish hair brushed up so that it was like new copper lit by electric light. Her face was broad, calm, and white. It was my sister who started me using the word "empty" about Nell's grey eyes. It was not the word I would have used myself, but her eyes did make me feel I was going to fall clean through them. When she looked up and saw me (my wash leather had squeaked on the pane), I nearly fell off the ladder. She took her hand from her ear so quickly that she knocked a scent bottle over, and at the same time she shut one of the drawers with her knee.

A man like Plushy, who upset some of the customers by singing non-stop while he worked, would have taken his comb out and run it through his hair and gone on singing. So he made out when I told him. It's a lie. He would have done just what I did. I opened the window and climbed in and said: "Sorry, miss. Let me wipe it up with the leather. If your old lady carries on, say it was the window cleaner."

She stood over me, looking insulted, and watched me wipe the scent off the carpet with the leather. The only thanks I got was: "Close the window when you go out. My Aunt Mary won't mind about the rug." I swear she said "My Aunt Mary," but afterwards she swore she didn't. The woman she worked for was misnamed Mrs. Merry—a gloomy lady in a houseful of books (I never saw so many), with a voice like a high-class ship going out to sea, very snobby—so I might have made a mistake. But it took a bit of time for me to get it into my mind that Nell was not the niece of this rich old bookworm.

Fate is a funny thing. Once it gets going, it never stops. I'd been working at different houses in the avenue for more than a year and I had never set eyes on Nell, but now I seemed to run across her one day after the other. I asked her if her aunt had been angry about the scent.

"No," Nell said. "She didn't mind. That's not my aunt. My aunt's in Manchester. I'm the maid."

I felt a fool trying to puzzle this out. Nell looked up and down the street, as if she were looking for someone. "I told her," she said. "She didn't mind."

"The lady you work for, you mean?" I asked.

"No, my Aunt Mary, in Manchester," she said. "I tell her everything."

I asked her to come out with me, but she changed her mood and said her aunt in Manchester would not like that, and neither would Mrs. Merry.

In those early days, it was always the same. This aunt of Nell's in Manchester wouldn't let her do anything. And to talk to Nell was like talking to two people, for she would turn her head aside when I said anything, as if she were discussing it with this old aunt of hers or someone else before she answered. I couldn't make out what age Nell was, either. To see her—short and solid and with her chin up, marching in slow, long steps down the street—she looked obstinate, like a schoolgirl; other times, when we were talking at a street corner, she had a small, disbelieving smile at the corner of her mouth, like a woman of thirty. She confused me. She was one person one minute and another the next. In the end, she said she would come out to the pictures with me, but I had to ask Mrs. Merry first.

I have said Mrs. Merry was like a ship. She bumped alongside her dining-room table when she came in, and docked at last in an armchair. Not in drydock: she was rocking a large glass of gin. She asked me a lot of questions about myself, my mother, and my sister, in a hooting sort of voice, and said Nell was a refined, quiet girl and that she didn't like her going out. "She is an orphan, you know," Mrs. Merry said loudly. "I understand her aunt brought her up. Very carefully—you can see. Her aunt in Manchester."

When Nell and I left the house, I could hardly speak for the idea that her Aunt Mary was walking beside us. And later I could pretty well feel her sitting beside us at the pictures. I got fed-up. We went to a milk bar afterwards, and Nell took her coat off. She showed me her bracelet and her wrist watch.

"Aunt Mary, I bet," I said.

"Yes," Nell said, with her nose in the air. "Aunt Mary." Her voice was small and soft, and seemed to me to come very clearly from a long way off.

There was no getting away from this aunt of hers. She lived in a huge house, Nell said, that had an enormous lawn in the shape of an oval, with a gravel path round it and a deodar at one end.

"What's a deodar?" I asked.

"A deodar? A tree," she said. "In the summer, she used to lie in a hammock under it. She taught me French." She was an educated girl; you could see that.

But I expect you're thinking what I was thinking: if Nell's aunt was so rich and classy, why was an educated girl like Nell down in this place working as an ordinary maid? I came straight out with it.

"No," said Nell. She began a lot of remarks with "No" when I asked her things. "There was trouble."

"You got into trouble?" I asked.

"No," she said. "Her husband did."

So Aunt Mary was married. She had got married only two years back, Nell told me. He was an elderly clergyman. I asked Nell what the trouble was. "It's private," she said. She just waved her hands. I had expected her to have broad, flat, strong hands, but they were small and plump; when she saw me looking at them, she put them in her lap and folded her fingers into her palms. But I had seen. She had a bad habit: she bit her nails.

I used to remember this when I got to taking her home to see my mother and sister.

"Class—that's all it is," my sister said. "Loaded down with Aunt Mary's jewellery and lying in bed all day long doing her face." She did not like Nell's lady-like accent.

One Saturday, after football, I told Plushy about Nell's Aunt Mary and the clergyman. "Do you reckon Nell's hiding something?" I asked him. "Has she been in trouble?"

"No," he said. "She just doesn't see the funny side."

"What's funny in it?" I asked.

"Clergyman," Plushy said.

So on Sunday I decided to get at it, and I asked Nell again about the clergyman.

"No," she said, in her usual way. "He was jealous of her giving me things. He had two children of his own. I couldn't stay after that. I can't bear jealousy."

"What was the clergyman's name?" I asked.

"No, you're going to cause trouble."

"How could I do that?"

"I don't know," she said. "You could. If you go and see him and tell him anything, I'll never speak to you again."

"I never want to hear the name of Aunt Mary again," I said. Then I calmed down. "What about you and me— you know—sort of getting fixed up, married?"

Nell was watching me as if I were trying to steal something from her. She sat there—we were sitting in a shelter by the sea—and she was two girls, one of them looking insulted. I oughtn't to have said that about her aunt. She got up and walked off. It was dark, and she didn't speak all the way home and she shook my hand off her arm when I touched it.

The next morning at eight o'clock she was outside our house. I went to the gate, and she ran and banged her head hard against my ribs, nearly knocking the wind out of me, and put her arms round me. She was crying. I took her in at the front door into our sitting room and told the others to keep away.

"She's dead," she said, sitting back from me. "Aunt Mary's dead. I told you a lie. She died last year. I couldn't bear her to be dead. She was going to look after me, and she left all her money—everything—to that clergyman. I didn't want her money, but I couldn't bear it. My father's dead, my mother's dead—I couldn't bear any more."

"There's me," I said. "Forget it."

"I told you a lie," she sobbed in my arms.

It wasn't long before Plushy came in and we were all laughing—my mother, my sister, even Nell.

"Blooming murderer," said Plushy when he heard it. "Look at him. No conscience. Kills a poor girl's auntie just to get his way."

"Shut up, Plushy," said my mother. "The girl's upset."

"It's easy for you, Ma," Plushy said. "But I was getting fond of Aunt Mary."

Nell gaped at him.

"Well, Nell," Plushy said. "He'll have to be your Aunt Mary now."

The Necklace

And so I was, for, except for some worry about where the clergyman had moved to and how he ought to do something for her—but all this was my mother's argument— Aunt Mary was a back number. Nell and I got married and we were on our own.

The rain stopped in the afternoon on that Saturday when I found the necklace. There was a lot of arguing when we got to the ground about whether we should play, because of the mess the field was in, and when we did start playing, it was a question of which side could stand up. Even chaps who were standing still suddenly fell down. The crowd was killing itself with laughter; you kicked the ball and you were flat on your back. Plushy and three others slid for yards into the Hopley goal and couldn't stop themselves; the Hopley goalie came out at them and went ahead first at Plushy. Their two heads cracked, wood against wood; you could hear it across the field. Plushy lost on this deal. It knocked him out for a few minutes. That is why, after the game, he went to the doctor's instead of coming home and having his tea with Nell and me, as he usually did.

I went back home alone. There was a change in Nell. She had done her ironing and she had put on her blue dress and she had done her hair. I don't mean that sort of change, though. She didn't often laugh, but now she came to me nearly laughing. She had the hot look of too much love. She even had some love left over for Plushy, and was very upset when I told her about him. She couldn't keep still. She rubbed against me like a cat when I sat down to tea, and then she leaned forward to me, pushing her plate nearer, looking at me while I was telling her about the game. Once or twice she interrupted me. "Sorry, I love you," she said.

I went on telling her about the game. Presently she sat back and said: "Haven't you forgotten something?"

She was smiling, but it was a heavy, greedy, large-eyed smile, as if her own natural smile had been made larger by a reflector.

"Have I left the bike out?" Sometimes I forgot to put the bike away.

"Think," she said. Since we had got married, she liked giving orders.

Slowly the smile went.

"No," she said shortly, and left the room. She really marched out of it. She went into the bedroom. I waited for her to come back, and when she didn't I called out: "I want some more tea!"

She did not answer. I pushed back my chair and went into the bedroom. She was standing at attention, with her back to me, in the middle of the room, doing nothing, with her hands at her sides. She did not turn round. Often when I didn't guess what she was thinking, she used to run off in in this way and stand in the next room, stiff and sulking. It would take a long time finding out what was the matter, for the only person she was on speaking terms with was herself. It happened a lot before we were married. But now, when she turned round suddenly, her face was half smiling and appealing. She was wearing the necklace.

When women put on something new, they look high and mighty, as if you had got to get to know them all over again. I don't like it. They also look ten years older. The pearls made Nell's neck look thick. They also made her look as if she wasn't married any longer, unless you could afford to pay the extra. I wished I was rich and could have bought pearls for her—well, not bought them myself, but sent her in somewhere to buy them. I don't like those shops.

She came toward me with half a clever tear in one eye. I call it clever; it wasn't real.

"Sorry, sorry," she said. "Don't be cross with me. I couldn't help it. The necklace fell out of your pocket. . . . It fell out of your pocket when I was putting your overalls away. I wasn't going through your pockets, I swear, if that's what you think. It fell out onto the bed." And she stepped to the bed and pointed to the place on the green quilt where it had fallen.

Some joke Plushy had once made about his landlady going through his pockets came back to me. For the first time, I knew that Nell had been going through my pockets on and off ever since we were married.

"Nell," I said, "that's not a present for you. I didn't buy it. I found it in the gutter in Alston Street, coming home, dinnertime. You thought it was for you."

"Who is it for?" she asked, all her newness going. "You found it—lying in the street?"

"It isn't for anyone," I said. "I don't know who it belongs to. We'd best take it to the police station."

"Police," she said, frightened.

"Yes," I said. "Some poor kid must have dropped it."

Her face hardened. "You weren't in Alston Street," she said. "You told Plushy you were in Hill Street. I heard you."

"No, I didn't," I said. "Plushy said that."

"No, tell me the truth. You're hiding something," she said. "Where did you find it?"

"Easy on," I said. "I told you. I found it in the gutter in Alston Street."

"Then why didn't you tell me? Hiding it in your pocket!"

"I wasn't hiding it. I just put it there."

"No, tell me the truth," she said again.

"I am," I said. "I'm going to take it round. I forgot it. Some poor kid's mother is carrying on, I bet."

"Her mother!" she said. "Whose mother? Jim, you've bought it for some girl." She put her hands to her neck, took the necklace off, and threw it on the bed. "Oh!" she cried out. "You've bought it for some girl! That's why you were hiding it!" And then she gave a howl and fell sideways on the bed, crying into the pillow, with her blue dress drawn up above her knees, and her legs coming out of it in a way so ugly and awful I could not believe it. I'd seen my mother do this once years ago, and, of course, I'd seen my sister do it often. She was a past master; the whole house stood still when my sister took a dive. But I thought it was the sort of thing that only went on in our family when I was a child. I said to myself: "So this is the girl whose aunt used to lie in a hammock under a deodar, talking French. Class—there's nothing in it!" I wished the time was two hours ago and I was playing football. I wished Plushy would come round.

"My tea's getting cold," I said after a bit. It must have been the way I said it. She sat up at once and came to the kitchen. She poured out the tea and sat down in front of me, and I liked her better with the necklace off, but her round face had become square and her white skin was thickly red down to her neck. Her mouth was as small as a penny. She had picked up the necklace and put it beside her plate.

"I'm waiting," she said.

"Plushy got hurt this afternoon," I said. "He got a crack on the head. You could hear it right across the field."

She did not answer for a long time, and then she said: "You told me that."

I remembered I had.

"How can you tell such lies?" she said. " 'Hear it across the field'! No, I'm sick of Plushy. Who are you married to? Is Plushy dead? I hope so."

"Oh dear, oh dear," I said.

"Stop talking like Plushy," she said. "Who is it for? Who did you buy it for? What's her name? I want the truth!"

"I've told you," I said.

"Aunt Mary warned me about you," she said.

"Your Aunt Mary never saw me," I said. "Aunt Mary's dead, anyway."

"Before she died," she said.

Aunt Mary had come back into our lives. It had been so long since we had even mentioned her or her husband that I could hardly remember who she was for the moment. I realized what a long way we had travelled since Aunt Mary's time, and I thought of what my mother had once said about how quickly the dead drop back into the past. But having her brought back like this from the grave, in this tone, woke up my old jealousy. I admit it; I was jealous of Aunt Mary.

"Please, Jim," Nell said, in a softer, pleading voice. "Who did you buy it for? Why did you do Hill Street this morning?"

So we went over the streets again: Launceston Road, the Promenade, Alston Street, across the High Street . . .

"You bought it at Cleaver's," she said.

"Learn some geography," I said. "I wasn't near Cleaver's."

"Learn it!" she sobbed. "That's all I do. I sit here all day thinking of where you are—one girl after another, just like Plushy."

"You're jealous," I said.

"Of course I'm jealous!" she shouted, in a thick, curdled voice like a man's.

"Now, look—" I said. I put my hand on hers, and she did not take it away. She turned her head from me and then said quietly, as though she were speaking to the necklace: "I know you found it, Jim. I'm sorry, I'm sorry."

I didn't say anything, and after a moment she said softly: "A valuable thing like that."

"It's just Woolworth trash," I said.

"Look at the clip," she said fearfully, handling the necklace to me. "It's worth hundreds."

"Get away!" I said.

"It is. I know it is," she said.

I picked up the necklace. The clip meant nothing to me, but, hearing her soft, truthful voice again, I felt sad. "Put it on again," I said. "You looked nice in it."

"Oh, I couldn't do that," she said. "It isn't ours."

"Go on. You put it on before. Let's see you. Just once more," I said. "It's yours," I said, laughing. I have explained she did not like jokes. She frowned. Then she leaned nearer to me but not looking at me—as if not to see me. "Jim," she said, in a very low voice. "You didn't find it in the street. Truthfully, you didn't did you? I won't say anything."

"What do you mean?"

The Necklace

"You knocked it off," she said.

The way she said this, as if she were whispering in my ear in the dark, frightened and excited me. Now she was searching my face for some hint or clue. There was a long silence between us.

I reached for the necklace and said: "I'm going round to the police with it now. I'm not a thief." But as I reached, there was a flash in her eyes and she snatched at it, too, as quickly as a cat.

"There'll be a reward!" she said, jumping up and standing away from me. We must have both caught the necklace, because it snapped and all the pearls scattered onto the carpet and over the lino. It was like during the war, when our corporal got his false teeth knocked out in the street. They went everywhere.

We were both down on our hands and knees at once. She was on the carpet. I was on the lino, by the dresser. This was how Plushy found us. There was a big piece of plaster on his forehead, under the curl of his black hair, where the goalie's head had cracked him.

"Don't step on them!" my wife called out.

"There's always something going on here," Plushy said.

"Stand still," we both said, straightening up.

"Let us pray," said Plushy, kneeling down, too. "What is it?"

Nell told him.

"Found it?" said Plushy sarcastically, getting up and standing above us. "What? Finds a necklace in the gutter with no neck in it! Doesn't tell his best friend!"

"Have you got the clip?" my wife asked me.

136

"Got a clip, too?" said Plushy. "Diamonds, I bet. Proper window cleaner's story. Lost your voice, Jim? Can't you sing?"

Nell reached up from the floor and put some of the pearls into a saucer.

"I bet he only whistles," Plushy said. "Whistling isn't strong enough. Jim, you know that, Whistling doesn't keep it off."

"Help us," said Nell. "Stop talking."

"Temptation," said Plushy, bending down to look. "By rights, I ought to be singing now, in case I slip one into my pocket. Remember old Charlie, Jim? He used to whistle like a canary. He was up someplace—Hill Street, twenty-seven. You know it, Jim—twenty-seven—don't put on that face with me. Charlie started whistling the moment he put the ladder up. Ground floor, he's whistling fine; first floor, O.K.; second floor, getting short of breath, whistle gets weak. What happens? Lady's diamond ring comes clean across from the other side of the room to him. He tries to blow it back. He can't. It comes clean through the glass. He can't get a sound out, leans back and back. Falls off the ladder, three weeks in hospital."

"Get on with the job, mate. Have you got the clip, Nell?" I said.

"I'm looking."

"I reckon singing's better. We always used to sing when we were working together, didn't we, Jim? Remember your lady, Nell, at the avenue?" Plushy put on the high-class hoot of Mrs. Merry. " 'Why doesn't someone stop that man singing?' Well, I did stop. I stopped right in the middle of a bar. Next thing, a five-pound note starts talking to me out of her handbag other side of the room and waving its hands about. Just like I'm talking to you now."

"Her watch, you mean," said Nell, getting up.

"Her watch?" said Plushy.

"Yes," said Nell. "I mean her watch. She missed a watch. I thought I'd never hear the last of it. Nothing funny about that, Plushy. I could have lost my place."

Plushy did not like this.

"What d'you mean, Nell?" I asked.

"It was all right. I found it for her," Nell said.

"Oh," said Plushy sarcastically. "That's something off my mind." Those two hated each other.

"We can't take it round like this," Nell said when we all stood up and looked at the saucer full of pearls. She dropped the clip on top.

"Too true you can't," said Plushy. "Looks too much like a ruddy share-out."

We argued about it for a long time. I was the only one in favor of taking it round and telling the police what happened. I did not want a valuable thing like this in the house, and we couldn't go round to Cleaver's or some place like that and get them restrung until Monday. It would be the end of the week before we could get them to the police.

"But Plushy's a witness," said Nell. "He'll tell them you found it and we broke it by mistake."

"Yes," said Plushy. "And you'll get a reward. What do I get?"

"Ten pounds," said Nell.

"Twenty," said Plushy. "First instalment on a motor bike. Pop up to London for the weekends."

"No. Aunt Mary's was worth hundreds," said Nell.

"Oh," said Plushy. "Got Nell's Aunt Mary back to stay with you?" he said to me. "You never told me. Is she comfortable? A bit cramped in here for her, isn't it?"

Nell put her chin up and looked like the geography teacher at our school when I was a boy. Nell really did hate Plushy, and getting a crack on the head had livened him up even more. He was a lad. We'd made Aunt Mary comfortable in the bath, according to him, or on top of a cupboard, and then he made up a long tale of how she wasn't getting on with the clergyman. His children got on her nerves and she wanted a rest, Plushy said. Nell struggled against it, and then she couldn't hold out any longer. She started to laugh. She laughed as I had never seen her, doubling up over the arm of a chair, and then, suddenly, she got angry. "Stop telling lies, Plushy!" she called out.

On Monday, Nell took the pearls down to Cleaver's to be restrung.

"Sit down, Mrs. Drayton," the older detective said to Nell, and the young one went out and came back in a moment with two cups of tea. When Nell came into any room where I was, the place was changed, and where I was, who I was, and what I was would get mixed up in my mind. It was like beginning to get drunk. Nell pushed the cup of tea away scornfully.

"It's just routine," the older one went on. "We've been asking your husband about the necklace you took round to Cleaver's to be restrung."

"It broke," I said.

"Just a minute, son," the detective said. And to Nell:

"Now, you say it is your necklace—your own property? Like you said to Mr. Cleaver: 'It is mine'? Is that correct?"

I had half got up from my chair and had tried to catch her eye when she walked in, but she came in warily, not looking at me but into each corner of the room and then up at the window and back at the door. I might have been a stranger. When she looked in my direction, she didn't see me; at any rate, she quickly turned her head to one side.

"That's correct," she said.

I think my mouth stuck wide open.

"Just a minute!" the young detective said to me sharply, shutting me up.

"But your husband says he found it at the corner of Alston Street and the Promenade," the other one said to her.

She looked at the young detective, then at the older one, then at me. I used to say that she confused me because she was like a couple of girls whispering secrets to each other, but now she was one woman, clear and decisive and firm in voice. There was nothing a long way off in it. It rang, and rang true and harsh.

"That's a bloody lie," said Nell.

"Nell!" I cried. I had never heard Nell use language before in my life.

"It's mine!" Nell shouted at me. "You know it is. Mr. Cleaver knows it is. I asked him what it was worth. He's repaired it for me before. He recognized it. It's been in my family for years. It belonged to my Aunt Mary. I told Mr. Cleaver. He knows. Bring him here. He knows it came to me when she died two years ago. She brought me up. Ask her husband, the Reverend Dickens. He lives in Manchester."

"Nell—" I said.

"What's the address of the Reverend Dickens?" asked the older detective.

"Find out. You're so bloody clever," said Nell. If she was more than one girl, I had never seen this one before—red and square in the face and her eyes moving like knife tips.

"Well," said the dick, "it's exactly like a necklace lost by a Mrs. Faber."

"Is it?" snapped Nell. "Well, it isn't hers. It's mine. It was my Aunt Mary's, I told you. She gave it to me. She gave me everything, all the things I have."

"Oh," said the detective. "Other things. What were they?"

"That's my business," said Nell.

"Mrs. Drayton," said the detective, "you haven't got an aunt, and you never did have, did you? Your father and mother live in London, don't they?"

"They're dead," I said. "Killed in the war. What's that got to do with it? Nell, what's going on?"

Nell suddenly took notice of me, as if she were seeing me for the first time. Her expression went through three changes. It was like seeing three photographs of a person quickly. The first was the square, raging face; the second lost its colour and softened; the third looked pale and sly. This one spoke to me in a low voice across the table, as if we were sharing a secret. "You silly sucker," she half whispered. "You're covering up for Plushy. I won't have Plushy."

141

The Necklace

And then she shouted at the detective: "Plushy whipped it off Mrs. Faber! Out with Plushy! Out! Out! My husband knows it." She got up and rushed for the door, but the young one was standing there.

I've left the window-cleaning trade now. I gave it up after the case. I had to. There was too much talk. Nell got three months. She was mad. She must have been: that's the only thing I can think. But she didn't look mad in court. She had just one word for all of us—the police, me, Plushy, old Cleaver, everybody: "Liars." The only straight people in the world were her and her Aunt Mary. It came out in court that she'd worked this Aunt Mary game a couple of times before she met me. Once in Deptford and another time at a place near Bristol. But for that she might have got off—first offence. "Her old auntie got round," Plushy whispered to me when the police were reading her record out to the judge. "Tiring, at her age."

The last I saw of Nell was going downstairs out of the dock with the wardress. She didn't even look at me. I couldn't believe it. I still can't believe it. My mind goes back to the first time I saw her, through the back-bedroom window at Mrs. Merry's, fixing the earrings—not hers but Mrs. Merry's—and I say to myself: "January eleventh we beat Hopley, three to nought," and I get stuck there.

Just a Little More

They were speaking in low voices in the kitchen.

"How is he? Has he said what he is going to do?" she asked her husband. "Is there any news?"

"None at all," the husband whispered. "He's coming down now. He says he just wants a house by the sea, in a place where the air is bracing and the water's soft and there's a good variety of fish."

"Sh-h-h! Why do we whisper like this? Here he comes. Get the plates."

A moment later the very old gentleman, her father-in-law, was standing in the doorway, staring and smiling. He was short and very fat, and one of the things he liked to do was to pause in the doorway of a room and look it over from ceiling to floor. In the old days, his family or his workers at the factory used to stiffen nervously when he did this, wondering where his eye would stop.

"Excuse me being rude," he said at last. "What a lovely smell."

"Take your father in," the wife said. "These plates are hot. Go into the dining room, Grandpa."

Just a Little More

"I'm just looking at your refrigerator, darling," the old gentleman said. "Very nice. It's a Pidex, I see. Is that a good make? I mean, is it good—does it work well? . . . I'm glad to hear that. Did you get it from the Pidex people? . . . Ah, I thought you did. Good people."

The son, who was in his fifties, took the old gentleman by the elbow and moved him slowly into the dining room. The old gentleman blew his nose.

"No. Your mother's hands were as cold as ice when I got to her," said the old gentleman, astonished by a memory. "But she had gone. Where do I go? Do I sit here?"

He sat down very suddenly at the table. Although he weighed close to two hundred pounds, his clothes hung loosely on him, for he had once weighed much more. His nostrils had spread and reddened over a skin that was greenish and violet on the cheeks but as pale and stringy as a chicken's at the neck.

His daughter-in-law and two grandchildren brought in the joint and the vegetables. The grandchildren were called Richard and Helen. They were in their teens. Their mouths watered when they saw the food on the table, and they leaned toward it, but kept their eyes politely on the old man, like elderly listeners.

"I hope you haven't cooked anything special for me," the old man said. "I was just saying I talk too much when I come for a weekend here, and I eat too much. It's living alone—having no one to talk to, and so forth, and you can't be bothered to eat—that's the point. What a lovely piece of beef that is! Wonderful. I haven't seen a joint of beef like that for centuries. A small bit of loin of lamb we might have, but my wife can't digest it." He often forgot that

144

his wife was dead. "And it doesn't keep. I put it in the larder and I forget and it goes wrong." His big face suddenly crinkled like an apple, with disgust.

"Well, well, I don't know, I'm sure," he went on, gazing at the beef his son was now carving. "I suppose it's all right. What do you call a joint like that?" He pointed across the table to his grandson. "We used to have beef when your father was a boy, Richard. Your father was a boy once. You can't imagine that, can you? Aitchbone, was it? I can't remember. I don't know where your mother used to get it. Bell's, I suppose. I don't know what we paid for it. Sixpence a pound, perhaps. We can't do it now: it's the price."

His son passed him a plate. The old man hesitated, not knowing whether to pass it on and not wanting to. "If this is for me, don't give me any more," he said. "I hardly eat anything nowadays. If I could have just a little fat . . ." Relieved, he kept the plate.

"Pass the vegetables to Grandpa," said his daughter-in-law to Helen.

"Grandpa, vegetables?" Helen said, looking younger now as she spoke.

"Oh," said the old gentleman. He had gone into a dream. "I was just watching you carving," he said to his son. "I was looking at your face. You've got just the expression of your great-grandfather Harry. I remember him when I was a little boy. Father took me to see him: it was one morning. He took me down to a warehouse, would it be?— in the docks or harbor—a factory, perhaps—and he lifted me up to a window and I saw him, just his face, it was only a minute. He was slitting up herrings. It was a curing place."

145

"Fish! I knew it." His daughter-in-law laughed.

"The sea is in our blood," said her husband. Everyone was laughing.

"What is this? What are you laughing at? What have I said?" the old gentleman asked, smiling. "Are you getting at me?"

"That is where you get your taste for kippers," said his daughter-in-law to her husband.

"Ah, kippers!" said the old gentleman, delighted by his strange success. "How are you for fish in this neighbourhood? Do you get good fish? I sometimes feel like a piece of fish. But there doesn't seem to be the fish about, these days. I don't know why that is. No, I went up to the fishmonger on Tuesday and I looked. He came up to me, and I said: 'Good morning.' 'Good morning, Mr. Hopkins,' he said. 'What can I do for you?' 'Do for me?' I said. 'Give me a fortnight in Monte Carlo.' He exploded. I said: 'What's happened to you? What's wrong?' 'What do you mean, Mr. Hopkins?' he said. 'I mean, where's your fish?' I said. 'That's not what I call fish. Not f–i–s–h.' He knew what I meant. 'Sole,' he said. 'Dover sole,' I said. 'Mr. Hopkins,' he said, 'I haven't had a Dover sole for a fortnight. Not one I'd sell *you*. Lemon sole,' he said, and something—greyling, did he say? Well, that's the way it is. And so we go on."

"No," the old man said after a moment. "Kitty, your mother, my wife, was very fond of fish. When we were first married, and so forth, we came down from the north—How old are you, my boy? Fifty-seven? You're not fifty-seven!— It was just before you were born, and my wife

146

said: 'I'd give anything for an oyster.' The train didn't get in till eight, but we were young and reckless in those days. I didn't care a damn for anyone. I was ready to knock the world over. I was in a good crib, five pounds a week at Weekley's—before Hollins took them over. All expenses. I thought I was Julius Caesar—marvellous, isn't it? Do I mean him? And we went across the road and your mother said: 'Come on—' "

The son interrupted, picking up the story. "And a bus driver leaned out of his cab and said: 'Watch out, lady. Babies are scarce this year.' Mother told me."

"I'm sure she didn't," said the old gentleman, blushing a little. "Your father's imagination, Richard!"

"Yes, but what happened?" asked his daughter-in-law.

"And there was a little place, a real old London fish place—sawdust on the floor, I suppose they had in those days. Crossfield . . . Cross . . . Crofty—I forget the name—and we had a dozen oysters each, maybe I had a couple of dozen; I don't remember now, I couldn't say. Frederick's—that was the name of the place. Frederick's. And I suppose we must have followed it with Dover sole. They used to do a wonderful Welsh rabbit."

"And that is how I was born," said the son. "Let me give you some more beef, Father."

"Me? Oh, no. I don't eat what I used to. It's living alone, and these new teeth of mine: I've had a lot of trouble with them. Don't give me any more. I don't mind a couple of slices—well, just another. And some fat. I like a piece of fat. That's what I feel. You go home and you get to the house, and it's dark. And it's empty. You go in and the

147

boiler's low: I don't seem to get the right coke. Do you get good coke here? You look at it all and you look in the larder and you can't be bothered. There's a chop, a bit of bread and cheese, perhaps. And you think, well, if this is all there is in life, you may as well finish it. I'm in a rut down in that place. I've got to get away. I can't breathe there. I'd like to get down to the sea."

"I think you ought to go where you have friends," said his daughter-in-law.

The old gentleman put his knife and fork down. "Friends?" he said, in a stern voice, raising his chin. "I have no friends. All my friends are dead." He said this with indignation and contempt.

"But what about your friend Rogers, in Devonshire?" said his son.

"Rogers? I was disappointed in Rogers. He's aged. He's let himself go. I hadn't seen him for twenty-five years. When I saw him, I said to him: 'Why, what's the matter with you? Trying to pretend you are an old man?' He looked at me. He'd let his moustache go long and grey. I wouldn't have known him. And there was something else. A funny thing. It upset me." The old gentleman's jolly face shrivelled up again, with horror. "The hairs in his nose had gone grey!" he said. "I couldn't bear it. He was very kind, and his wife was. We had lunch. Soup of some kind—tomato, or maybe oxtail—and then a piece of lamb, potatoes, and cauliflower. Oh, very nice. I've forgotten what the dessert was—some cream, I suppose, they have good cream there—and coffee, of course. Cheese . . . I don't remember. Afterwards—and this is what upset me about old people—they wanted a rest. Every day, after lunch, they go off and have a sleep—every day. Can you imagine that? I couldn't stand that. Terrible."

"It's good to have a siesta," said the son.

"I couldn't. I never have. I just can't," said the old gentleman, in a panic. "The other afternoon after lunch—I forget what I had, a chop, I think—I couldn't be bothered to cook vegetables—well, on your own you don't, that's the point—I dropped off. I don't know how long, and when I woke up it was dark. I couldn't see anything. I didn't know where I was. 'Where am I?' I said. 'What day is it?' And I reached out for my wife. I thought I was in bed, and I called out: 'Kitty, Kitty, where are you?' and then I said: 'Oh.' It came back to me. I'm here. In this room. I couldn't move. I got up and put on the light. I was done up. I poured myself out a small glass of port. I felt I had to. It was shocking. And shocking dreams."

He stared and then suddenly he turned to his daughter-in-law and said, in another voice: "Those sandwiches I shan't forget. Egg, wasn't it? You remember." He wagged a finger at Helen. "Helen, your mother is a wonder at egg sandwiches. It was the first time in my life I'd ever eaten them. The day we put Kitty away, you remember she came down and made egg sandwiches? What is the secret of it? She won't tell. Butter, I suppose? Richard, what is the word I want? You know—'smashing,' I suppose you'd call them."

He paused, and his eyes grew vaguer. "No," he went on, "I don't know what I'll do. I think I shall go to the sea and look round. I shall get a list of houses, and put my furniture in store. I could live with your brother, John, or you. I know I could, but it would be wrong. You have your own lives. I want my independence. Life is beginning for me—that is what I feel. I feel I would like to go on a cruise round the world. There was a house at Bexhill I saw. They wanted seven thousand for it. I felt it would suit me."

"Seven thousand!" said his son, in alarm. "Where would you get seven thousand from?"

"Oh," said the old gentleman sharply, "I should raise it."

"Raise it!" exclaimed the son. "How?"

"That's just it," said the old gentleman cheerfully. "I don't know. The way will open up. You, perhaps, or John."

Husband and wife looked down at the table at each other in consternation.

"Shall we go upstairs and have some coffee?" she said.

"That son of yours, that Richard—did you see what he ate?" said the old gentleman as he got up from the table. "Marvellous, isn't it? Of course, things are better than when I was a boy. I feel everything is better. We used to go to school with twopence for a pie. Not every day—twice a week. The other days, we just looked at the shop window. Pies piled up. And once a week—Friday, I expect—it was herrings in the evening. The fisherwoman came calling them in the street, eighteen a shilling, fresh fish out of the sea. Salmon, I used to be fond of. D'you ever have salmon?"

He paused in the doorway and looked at the carpet on the stairs and at the wallpaper. "I like rich things," he said, nodding to the carpet. "That gravy was good. Luscious grapes, pears, all large fruits I like. Those Christmas displays at the meat market—turkeys and geese by the thousand there used to be. I always used to bring your mother something. A few chops, two or three pairs of kippers. And so forth. I don't know what."

"Upstairs to the sitting room, Father," said the son. "I'm coming in a minute with the coffee."

The son went into the kitchen, and the whispering began again.

"Seven thousand!" he said. "Seven million wouldn't keep him!"

"Sh-h-h," said his wife. "It's a day-dream."

"But what are we going to do?"

In a few minutes, he took the coffee upstairs. The old gentleman was sitting down, with his waistcoat undone and his thumbs twiddling on his stomach.

"I've been thinking about you," the old gentleman said rebukingly. "You've lost weight. You don't eat. You worry too much. My wife used to worry."

The son passed a coffee cup to him.

"Is there a lot of sugar in it? Thank you," the old man said. He gave it a stir, took a sip, and then held the cup out. "I think I'll have a couple of spoonfuls more."

The Snag

The marriages of middle age, the mad impromptus of reason, are the satisfying ones. By that time our obsessions have accumulated and assert their rights, and we find peace in the peculiarities of others. I am thinking of Mrs. Barclay and myself. Our difficulty was the common one of turning a love affair into a marriage.

Sophia was a rattled woman of forty, with a pretty nose, when I met her. We had both gone to Percy Oblong's wedding party in Holland Park. She belonged to that set. Until I was crushed into a corner with her in one of the crowded rooms, and questioned her, I knew hardly any of the guests. There were, it seems, several important politicians, two or three titles, actors, actresses, authors; a large number of people known to the glossy magazines and, of the rest, there were scarcely any—according to the lively Mrs. Barclay—without some well-known tale attached to them. It was Percy's third marriage and she pointed out to me that a feature of the party was its half-dozen youngish women who had known Percy too well and were prowling about with champagne glasses in their hands and with beautiful expressions of perturbed wistfulness, rather ostentatiously breathing out the news that emotional fulfilment had come to them after—thank God—giving Percy up. They were saying, as Sophia did, that he looked fatter. Among people shouting to be heard as the packed evening went on, Sophia's animated and gloomy mumble was refreshing and audible. We were both looking for a chance to get away from each other, when suddenly she pulled my sleeve so hard that I almost fell on her.

"Don't move," she said sharply. "Don't go. Stand still. Stand there. Talk. There's someone I don't want to see. Don't turn round."

That is what started it—I mean started our affair. A conspiracy had begun. I was at once attracted to her. I asked her who she was hiding from and she said she would tell me later. The danger did not abate, and the longer it lasted, the more attractive I found her. Eventually I was offering to spy out the land. Then I had to get her out of the corner, out of the room, down the stairs, out of the house. The manoeuvre was a triumph. As we stood in the cool black damp of the London night I knew that I had found at last my real gift. I was a rescuer. Fatal discovery. I got a taxi and took Sophia back to her flat and that evening, and in the weeks that followed, I discovered calamity was what she lived by.

I shall always remember Sophia's flat. All day and half the night it rattled with the sound of electric trains; and all day and half the evening the telephone rang in it. She lived among a lot of expensive art books and pictures of the ballet and in a luxury that betrayed the deserted woman who had wrung out of interior decoration the things that she had failed to get from marriage. But the whole place shook. And her life—as she took pride in confiding—shook too. Never missing a party, eager to be at the centre of other people's love affairs and, she admitted, careless about her own, she was the centre of a lot of gossip. My instincts as a rescuer became stronger and stronger. Two months after Percy Oblong's wedding I was talking of the supreme act of life-saving: marriage. Sophia, between telephone calls, responded warmly to this idea; for her, it had the lure of suicide. But there was an obstacle. She had been divorced in a noisy way, many years before—she could quote from the papers and remembered what she wore in court—and to this divorce she clung. It had sacred implications. She behaved about it like a cautious widow whose little capital was this shaming and perfect disaster. "You have not been divorced," she said. She meant that I had no disaster of my own to put into a settlement.

And here we stuck, talking and talking, and the trains went by. And then, my luck turned. Calamity occurred. The seeds of it had been sown at our first meeting. Six months after that scene at Percy Oblong's wedding, in a week when I was away, Sophia landed herself with a slander action. Her telephone calls were all law and lawyers. She spoke lines that could have been convincing only on the stage. Nothing I could do when I came back could stop her, and for three farcical days the British public were laughing about "the Barclay case." I saw this was the supreme test. Here was the dramatic setting we needed. Sophia was ill. She was frightened by what she had let herself in for. "I must get her out of the limelight," I thought. "I must save her, restore her reputation." I talked her down and took action. She surrendered. It was August. I found a cottage in Wales where we could escape for a month. The Monday after the case I went up to get it ready. On the Wednesday I was to return to London and fetch her and we were to get married.

The cottage was a simple, cream-painted gate lodge with sharp Gothic windows. It was darkened by one of those tall firs that are often seen in rectory gardens and that are sometimes called "clergyman trees." One felt almost married standing under it. There was one advantage in the place from my point of view: it had no telephone. In our London days, Sophia's telephone had been my malignant rival, for Sophia lived by it. A few hours before returning to London to fetch her and on the day when I considered myself to be officially "running away with Mrs. Barclay," a boy arrived with a telegram from her. It told me to wait because she had decided to drive up to me. I had forgotten about telegrams. I saw that now I was not, in the strictest sense, "running off with Mrs. Barclay." The struggle for power had begun.

And so I see her as she was, on that day, driving towards me in the Border country. Sophia was a single-minded driver, but the mind she used was the unconscious. I see her green car unpredictable in the traffic lanes, waltzing at corners. I hear her shouted at by other motorists, I see her chancing the yellow light, parking in the wrong place at Cheltenham, backing into the traffic stream at the narrow end of Worcester, making cyclists swerve. She had a small pink hat half hidden in her hair, at an angle that gave her pale face the look of folly the waning moon has in a windy sky. I could imagine the restlessness of her pretty and conversable shoulders. I did not know what to do with myself until two o'clock when she was to arrive, and the changeable August sun made the hours slower. Over and over again

The Snag

I looked at flowers I did not know the name of in the garden. That tedium was broken. Telegrams began to arrive as suddenly as telephone calls. Two came from London, altering the time of departure. One came from Kidderminster saying she had taken the wrong road. And a final one from a town in Shropshire telling me to ring the hotel. I drove to the nearest telephone box.

"My dear," she said with her low, fussed, guttural emphasis on the second word. "Avoid me. Keep out of my way. I am poison. Ugh."

I could imagine her shaking her head in a disgust with herself which used to please me.

"You know what has happened? It is unbelievable. Tyre burst!" She added that there was an awful man in shorts staring at her.

This, I knew, would be untrue. While she was telephoning, Sophia would be regarding the man in shorts. Her ice-blue eyes would be staring in a rude, incredulous way; she was hypnotized by the sight of men, of terrible men. I suppose I describe myself.

"Stay where you are," I said. "Don't worry. Rest. I will come and fetch you."

"Yes," she said. "I must rest. I'm half dead."

It took me no more than half an hour to drive to the town. She was in the white lounge. She was wearing a grey suit and was sitting, slim and very upright, with a silk scarf round her long and beautiful throat, and she was wearing the foolish hat on her greying hair. She was looking severely amused, but when she saw me, she put all her vanity into a deep, laughing groan.

"My dear," she said in an exhausted voice when she took

my hand. Her hand was small, nervous, and brittle, as if it would break.

"You're a saint. What is it that happens to me? I wreck everything. Why did I take that wrong road at Kidderminster? What *made* me?"

We were neither of us any longer young. Explanations were a game that gave us the illusion of youth and made our troubles and our past sparkle. We had grown up at the time when simplicity went out.

"You were trying not to come," I said.

That kind of remark delighted her. It pleased me too. We felt younger. A belief in fate was her form of hypocrisy.

"Have you had tea? If you have, let's go. I've got my car," I said.

"In two cars?" she said. "Don't be silly. You see what a muddle it is. We must talk."

"Not," I said, "with all these people. They are too interested. And why talk?"

"Look at them," she said. "I can't believe it."

We were sitting in a zoo. The lounge of the hotel smelt of white paint, of tea, of new carpet and roses, and there was a long beam of sunny-blue cigarette smoke slanting between us and one of the sofas. Arranged in their armchairs were a number of what looked like dressed-up animals. There were giraffes, tigresses, monkeys, birds, dogs, and even a camel; they were middle-aged ladies, knitting or reading, and acutely interested in human nature—that is to say, Sophia and me. The only persons not listening to us had their backs to us. There was a man on the sofa beyond the beam of smoke with strong grey hair as thick as a schoolboy's. Near him sat a youth of sixteen wearing a school blazer and flannels. He wore spectacles. Of the man I could see only the sunburned neck and the shoulders of his tweed jacket. The youth was gazing at Sophia and turned his head, blushing, when I caught his look. He had a red notebook on his knee.

The man had a book, too. Suddenly he slapped it on his knee and said in a ringing and confident voice:

"We're absolutely stumped, old boy."

The zoo looked up from their knitting needles.

"Ssh!" said Sophia to me. "Listen. It's fascinating. It's the man I told you about—the one in shorts who was staring at me."

"Umph!" said the boy in a voice that was far more elderly than the man's.

"He's a professor or something," Sophia said. "Anyway, he knows a lot of women professors. He's on holiday. That is his son. They're on a bus tour. He was looking at me as if he knew me."

"You are not a woman professor," I said. "How d'you know all that?"

Sophia was annoyed by this; she seriously liked to be whatever was going, if a man were concerned.

"He's been telling us all. Listen," she said.

"That boy will know you again," I said.

Sophia stared back at the boy in a prim and amused way that crushed him once more.

The man cleared his throat and the boy said something to his father obviously about us. The father spoke again. He was making a speech to the room. The pitch of his voice was exacting. It was the good-humoured voice of a humourless man, questing, inflected by a note that blended educated anxiety with the exhilaration that is shared by sea lions and great bores. It was a voice both specifically victimizing and blandly generic. It was the voice of a university.

"The twenty-sixth," it said. "That's where we're sunk."

"No bus," the boy said.

"Let's have a look at your book again," said the father. Sophia sighed.

There was a pile of guidebooks and timetables on the table beside the boy among the magazines. He handed the red notebook to his father.

"I don't see," said the father, opening the book and turning the pages, "how we've slipped up. We've done exactly what we planned." He took a pencil and ticked pages of the book, item by item. " 'August sixteenth. Leave Trigorin eight fifteen, arrive Llandor eleven thirty, Church, museum, sandwiches. Stay George and Dragon'—all right?"

He ticked these items in the book.

" 'August nineteenth'," he continued. " 'Leave nine'— What's this? I can't read your writing. You must learn to write figures in a clear, uneducated hand—ha! ha! I can't tell whether this is a three or a five. . . ."

"Five," said the boy. "We've done that."

"I know, I know," said the father. "But I like things right. We may want to look this up in years to come. Now. Nine five." He altered the figure. The boy looked towards us with shame.

" 'August nineteenth'," said the father. " 'Leave Llandor, arrive Creep eleven twenty. Visit castle, query dungeon.' Yes, we did the dungeon. 'Early lunch Globe, another castle, bus two o'clock to Bronwen, waterfall, tea, stay Crown . . .' "

"That poor boy," I said.

"There's a lot more, the whole holiday," said Sophia. "Day by day. Why poor? That's exactly what one ought to do."

"Well, his poor wife," I said. "I can't see you doing it."

"That's where you're wrong," Sophia said. And then: "She's not with them. She's dead."

The certainty of Sophia made me laugh.

"Obviously she's dead," she said, and there was that dry, seductive, low-spirited choke in her throat, that grimace of ironical horror, that small, practical, disposing movement of the chin which indicated that Sophia was facing a decisive and agreeable interment.

Sophia's words made me look more closely at the man. I picked up a magazine and looked over the top of it. I stopped smiling. Now I knew why I had noticed a peculiar quality in his voice. It was not generic. It was specific. I knew him. His wife *had* died. She had died three years before. It was a man called Charles Chaucer. I whispered this to Sophia.

"Ssh!" she said. "Listen."

"I know him," I repeated. "It is Charles Chaucer."

Sophia paid no attention. She was listening to Chaucer, who was still speaking.

Rather than dismay, I felt laughter rise through my feet and grow inside my body, getting deeper and deeper until I was submerged in it. Sophia believed in Fate and so did I. But my notion was different from hers. Her belief enabled her to make a devious escape into a melancholy that permitted her to get out of anything she wanted to get out of. For me, I had only to look at Chaucer: Fate was the asinine. At forty-five I found my cheeks burning because the world's oldest joke was being played on me and, as always, at the time of crisis. To have met anyone at this moment would have been awkward. To meet Chaucer was farce.

For a little while I thought of getting away unseen. I studied the room. There was only one door in the middle. I had come in by this door unseen, else Chaucer would have sprung at once. There was no escape. I put down the magazine and stared at Chaucer's neck, daring him to look round.

Chaucer was farce because he was what is called my "oldest friend." I do not mean that he was a friend in any serious sense. His role in life was to be the oldest friend of everyone, the man who crops up in one's life on and off for twenty years and always at the unguarded moments. At Dieppe when one is sneaking out; at Dover when one is sneaking happily back. It is his knock at the door that stops the domestic quarrel, that interrupts the love affair or makes one put the pistol back in the drawer. Chaucer arrived in my life, every few years, like a clown or a conscience, innocently, creating guilt. His innocence lay in his efficiency in pursuing the single purpose of his life: "I like to keep in touch." The kiss is killed; the suicide misses his moment. Chaucer saves us.

"And you see what the twenty-sixth means," Chaucer was saying. "I can't believe that they don't run a bus every day, but here it is as plain as anything. Thursdays only. What a day to run a bus, anyway. It's a real headache."

The Snag

The boy murmured.

"The snag is," Chaucer said, "that it knocks Snowdon clean out."

He said this as if he had brought the whole mountain down on top of himself.

The idea of Snowdon, the highest mountain in England, being "knocked clean out" made several ladies in the lounge look with the *de haut en bas* expression of English unbelief. There were snobbish smiles, but two ladies looked at Chaucer with sympathy. One of these was Sophia.

But there Snowdon rose implacably out of Chaucer's timetable, a mountain not subject to the climbing boots of poets like the mountains of the Lake District, not fatal to clerks like Ben Nevis, but well clambered by lawyers, doctors, professors, and undergraduates, injuring its half-dozen, even killing its occasional woman schoolteacher, every year, often in the headlines, sold to publicity. It rose out of Chaucer's timetable in the drifting Welsh rain, encircled by teams of cyclists, belted by motor coaches; the steep side falling into cones of scree, the sheep bleating like Wesleyan ministers on the gentler slopes, the farmers glowering at the tourists over the stone walls at the bottom, and the excursions from Manchester going up the long slope on foot or by the light railway to the café in the inevitable cloud at the summit. There they waited for the famous view, while the professional classes were roped on the chimney or the rock face. It stood there rather wet, very lordly in its rock, hostile to Chaucer's passion for contact.

"We'll have to miss it," the boy said in a false voice.

The sympathetic lady and Sophia, too, looked sorry for the boy.

"Miss it!" cried the dogged Chaucer. "But we can't miss
Snowdon."

"Suppose we make it Wednesday," said the boy.

"No good," said the father, looking at the timetable. "The
eleven twenty misses the connexion by a quarter of an
hour."

"No co-operation," said the boy.

I changed my mind. This seemed the moment to slip
out.

"Darling," I said, "let's go."

"All right," said Sophia with resignation.

"Unless . . . unless," said Chaucer. "Here's an idea.
Wait. Let me think."

Sophia had moved and the boy now gasped as if he were
about to miss the biggest chance of his life. Agitatedly he
tried to attract his father's attention. In the silence of Chaucer's thinking I heard the boy mutter.

"Dad! Dad! That's the woman in the Barclay case."

"Damn!" I said. "That boy reads the papers."

"Where?" said Sophia, looking round the room. She was
paying no attention to me.

"Just a moment," said Chaucer. "I think I've got it. We
don't go to Canwer, we take the early bus." (I did not
catch the name of the place.) "Look at the timetable."

The boy rummaged among the books but did not take
his eyes off Sophia.

"We can't do that," said the boy.

"We can. We can," cried Chaucer. "Why go to the *top* of
Snowdon? We can work it if we go halfway up. What's
wrong with that? Snowdon, halfway," he declared. "That's
the idea."

163

The Snag

There was a sigh from the snobbish ladies. They were satisfied. The gentler ones saw the wish to protect Chaucer made irrelevant. Sophia, who had been rapt and ironical, made her grimace and was suddenly set in the gloom I feared in her. I squeezed her hand.

"What's the *good* of going to the top, old boy? What's the point?" said Chaucer. "It's no different from other mountains. You get much the same view halfway."

"O.K.," said the boy, getting out his pencil.

Chaucer sat forward on the sofa, elated.

"The important thing in life is to ask the right questions," he said.

Sophia sat back and picked up the magazine and leaned towards me. Looking at the advertisement of a fur coat, she said:

"How right he is! I've been going to the top, going to the limit all my life. Why? It is just as good halfway. That's why I am such a mess. I mean—take the case. Why did I go on with it? Why didn't you stop me?"

"I tried to," I said. "But there's no stopping you, you know, once you're set. You're stubborn."

"I need someone to stop me," she said. "You know who that man is?"

"I have just been telling you. It's Chaucer."

"Don't be silly. I'm serious," she said. "It's my husband, to the life."

We were back where we had so often been before—to the sacredness of Sophia's divorce.

"Listen," I said. "I'm telling you. It's a man called Chaucer, a friend of mine. I know him. What do we do now?"

"Oh, no!" she exclaimed, opening her handbag and getting out her mirror. "Why on earth didn't you tell me! Let's go and speak to him. What an extraordinary man you are."

At this the unmistakable voice of my oldest friend spoke out.

"The Barclay case? Why didn't you tell me? Where?"

Chaucer stood up and recognized me at once. His face was as pink as his neck. His blue eyes shone.

"How absolutely splendid," he cried.

We went to him at once; Sophia still had the magazine in her hand as I introduced her.

"Marvellous," said Chaucer. "This is my son."

Chaucer's face did not astonish me. It was young; it was sunburned to the neck. What astonished me was his clothes. Perhaps because of the mild youthfulness of his face, they seemed to overpower and astonish and magnify him. A stupendous tropical butterfly in tweed had broken out of the chrysalis of mourning. I had never seen this Chaucer before. Fresher and even younger after grief, he now wore a blatant black, red, and green jacket in wide check. A blue-and-white-checked open shirt seemed to boil on his chest, and a few chest hairs showed like a whiff of steam at the neck. His khaki shorts made his pink knees look wilful, like smooth supernumerary faces, tripling his powers of observation; the dark-red stockings with the green scout tabs to the garters added a Tyrolean friskiness. In his ordinary crisis get-up he had been a grey figure. Now he was sporting and as blatant as a poster. A desire for publicity had been submerged in him.

"How d'you do?" he was saying to Sophia, holding her hand and turning to his son to say: "Janet Forth was here this afternoon, wasn't she, old boy? You remember?" (This to me) "She was up at Newnham and went to the Foreign Office until she left for Athens—the British school. Got a C.B.E.—did you know? You've only just missed her."

At least we had not been his first prey that day.

"Took a first in history," he went on to Sophia, at last releasing her hand. "Sit down," he said. "This is splendid."

We did not sit down.

"Trust C.C.," I said to Sophia, "to remember the learned ladies."

Chaucer laughed shyly and innocently, giving Sophia a look that searched her face for her academic distinction. For Chaucer was Don Juan—but not the ordinary version of that character. He was the pursuer of academic women. To their persons and their sex he was indifferent: his lust and single-minded quest was for their intellectual particulars. Where had they been to school? To which university? In what year? With whom? When had they got their degrees? In what subjects? Had they taken a first or a second? A large procession of educated women had given their academic all to Chaucer's amorous mind. Some had even become Dames. He sent blue-eyed glances at Sophia, who suddenly became gay. What small academic jewel did she possess? An intermediate, perhaps? A mere diploma? It was an academic undressing. I grinned. There was not a trace of intellect, beyond the usual socialite pickings, in Sophia. If she had graduated anywhere it was in the courts —the Divorce Court and the Queen's Bench. Her only distinction was public scandal. Chaucer's son, standing back and unable to close his mouth, knew that. He was overcome.

In the meantime, Chaucer was eagerly telling us what we knew already.

The Snag

"Snowdon," he said. "We've run into a spot of bother there. I thought of dropping in on Mary Cumberland. . . ."

He was off again on his quest. He gave me a knowing look as he drew once more on the notorious provender of his power to bore. Then, without warning, he said genially to Sophia:

"My son was just telling me he was sure he knew you. He saw your picture in the papers . . . the Barclay case."

I could not speak. The son could not speak. All the ladies in the room—the giraffe, the dogs, the tigress, and the camel —put down their books and stared.

"I expect he did," Sophia said. "It was everywhere. Which one did you see?" She put this question to the boy.

She was delighted and proud and radiant; and there was a pout of reproach at my annoyed face. I was depriving her of the only gain the case had brought her: publicity.

"I got my damages," she said impudently with a new defiant look at me.

"I know. A farthing," said the boy, an addict of fact.

Sophia saw my fidgeting shame. She knew the damages were contemptuous and that the case had been a calamity to her reputation.

"Splendid!" Chaucer said to her in his eager, pointless way. She was even more pleased. She turned to look at the ladies in the lounge and for a long time I had not seen her eyes so brilliant or heard her answering voice so vivacious. For myself, my worst memories of the scene in court were re-enacted. I expected to hear the judge, who looked like some moralizing old woman in a red bathrobe and curlers— I expected to hear the judge say again:

"You may think the defendant is a woman of evil mind,

167

The Snag

. . . On the other hand you may think that Mrs. Barclay is not a woman for whom discretion means very much and that she has shown a general disposition to meddle and to make much of very little. You have seen her in the witness box. You may ask if she is to be relied upon. . . ."

And I could hear myself saying to Sophia before the action:

"Leave it alone. The woman is a spy. She has got her friends to watch you. People like that destroy themselves. Let them. It can't hurt you."

"Unelevating society . . . frivolous action . . . storm in a teacup . . . ill-advised ladies . . ."

I could hear the judge going on. His voice melted into the voice of Chaucer, who never dropped a piece of research.

"Who was the judge?" he asked.

Sophia told him.

"He was up at Magdalen with me," cried the ecstatic Chaucer, rumpling the rug at his feet.

Sophia liked a social titbit like that. She would have gone to the scaffold with pleasure if, on the way, she could have picked up a bit of gossip about the hangman. Her pleasure and Chaucer's were complete.

"Now tell me about your holiday," she said to the boy. "Let me see your marvellous book."

She rummaged among the magazines and soon had the table in disorder. She found his notebook.

"Ah, this is where you write it all down. What a good idea," she said. "You like to have everything planned."

The boy was ashamed.

"Dad does," said the boy.

"So do I," said Sophia.

I gaped at her.

"I wish I wrote everything down," she said. "You know where you are. There is nothing to worry about. You've got it all except for one day." She changed her lively manner and her argument. "Isn't it rather thrilling? Not knowing? I mean unless you'd planned all the others, this one wouldn't be so thrilling."

The youth looked suspiciously at her.

"Now, then, you two," said Chaucer. "Sorry to break it up."

Chaucer's face was so sunburned, his son's face so pale, that he looked as if he had taken all the sunshine of their holiday for himself; now he was taking Sophia's kindness. I was relieved that it was he who was breaking up our meeting. I feared it would last for ever.

"En route," he said to his son. "Leave the books there. Five thirty. We've just got time for the castle. Let's meet later on at dinner."

I murmured something and they went.

"I hope not," I said to Sophia. She was looking for her magazine in the muddle she had made on the table. She picked it up.

"Now," I said. "I suppose that was all right."

"Let's sit down," she said. Her gaiety had gone. "I feel so low."

"Those clothes of his. That suit! I love you," I said.

We sat down where Chaucer had been sitting. The seat was warm with him still.

"What about his clothes?" said Sophia. "You men are sweet. Straighten the rug, my dear. Did you see him, how he drew the rug up between his feet when he was talking to us?

I was fascinated. He had almost worked it up to his knees in a heap. Is he always confident like that?"

"I didn't notice," I said. "That wasn't confidence: it was nerves."

"Oh no! I could not look at anything else. I can't bear men who stand still," she said.

I straightened the rug.

"You did not tell me he was your oldest friend," she said.

"He isn't," I said. "But I have always known him."

I gave her my reflections on oldest friends. She did not laugh.

"How little I know about you," she said. "You don't really know me."

"We've known each other a long time," I said.

"Nearly a year," she said. "He's like my husband."

"Yes—you said. That was a bit of shock, you know. Did he live on the examination papers of female dons?"

"Certainly not," said Sophia, flashing in defence of her husband. "Remember, I've been married. You have not."

"I'm glad for your sake."

"Why for mine?"

"You might have been jealous," I said.

"Are you?" she said.

Sophia's husband had been a bond between us. His gratifying stupidity, his dullness, his baldness, his obstinacy had convinced me of my power over all the gossip about her. I had failed, of course, to stop her from going on with the silly slander action and I was put out by the scene with Chaucer, which had shown me that, unrepentantly, she enjoyed the fight for its own sake and expected to be admired for it.

What disturbed me was that Sophia's husband was an abstraction no longer. He was real. Possibly he wore a loud sports jacket and shorts and said things like "Absolutely splendid."

"Darling," I said. "I did not come here to sit in this hotel but to take you home. We are going to be married."

"My dear," she said, drawing away. "We must talk."

"Talk," I said. "What for? What about? We've done all the talking. I said . . . marry."

She took my hand and squeezed it.

"I'm worn out," she said. "I'm so bewildered. I feel so numb."

"We shall be quiet and peaceful," I said.

"Peace—how I want it," she said.

"Look, I'll see about your car and we'll go home."

"I'm terribly sorry," she said. "This is not what I intended but I'm utterly whacked. I haven't slept for nights. And then Kidderminster . . ."

"Now, you've told me about Kidderminster. I'll go and see about the car."

"My dear," she said. "I can't. It wouldn't be fair."

"What do you mean?"

"I'll be better in the morning," she said hurriedly. "It's just the journey and we must talk."

"Talk?" I said with exasperation.

"I promise you, in the morning," she said. "I'm going to stay here tonight. I've got a room. I'm sorry."

"Sophia!"

She became very pale.

"I know," she said. "Forgive me."

"But I've got the cottage. You let me get the cottage

ready." I was angry. "When did you get a room here?" I asked. "If you stay, I stay."

"Oh no, you can't do that," she said in a prudish fluster that I always found attractive. "It wouldn't do."

She looked nervously at the row of women in the room. "You mustn't."

"Darling," I said. "I love you. You've come all this way to love me."

"You did not come to London for me," she said.

"Darling! Your telegram," I said. "You told me not to."

"Did I? Do you always do as you are told? Darling, your face. It looks so tragic. Don't, please, look like that. I can't bear it. It's only women, my dear. Oh lord, I'm always doing this."

"Always?" I said sharply.

Her husband had become real. Now all the scandals became real also. The judge returned in his red bathrobe.

"Unreliable . . . frivolous . . ." he was still saying.

She listlessly picked up her magazine and she looked at me.

"I'm telling you the truth," she said. "Do you think I tell you the truth, always?"

"Yes," I said. Afterwards, very often afterwards, puzzling about this question of hers, I remembered a movement of her lower lip when I answered. It was a movement of disappointment. She wanted me to say that I knew she was telling a lie. She badly wanted to be seen through, but despair had made me blind.

"I'm going to get the car," I said decisively and, getting up, walked out of the lounge into the hall and asked for the name of the garage. I was not away for more than a quarter of an hour.

When I came back she had gone. She had left a message with the hall porter saying that she would ring me in the morning.

"Madam said she was feeling tired," said the porter in a voice of pious intimacy.

"Give me the telephone."

"There are no telephones in the rooms," he said with pride.

Sophia and I had certainly moved into a different world.

The man gave me her room number and, with disapproval, watched me walk up the shabby stairs. Her room was number 8 on the first floor. I went up, crossed a landing that contained the largest case of stuffed seabirds I had ever seen. It gave a dead marine odour to the passage. I knocked. The door opened and there stood Chaucer.

"Splendid, man!" cried Chaucer. "Come in. We're just back. Where's Mrs. Barclay? Let's all go and have a drink."

I looked at the number of the door. It was 18. The 1 had been badly defaced.

"She's gone to bed very tired," I had the resource to say. "I'm just going home."

Chaucer gave me a sly look that only the professional oldest friend can give. He knows the world is full of happenings he can only be on the edge of. He conveys: "Between us it is unnecessary to say anything, but I think you are being very unwise."

"She's in number eight," he said enthusiastically. "I looked it up if you want her."

"No, no. I'm just going home," I repeated.

"Well, then, one for the road. You must," he said.

He marched me down the stairs.

"There's meeting you to celebrate," he said at the bar. "So many years . . ." he said. "Not," he said with a killing blue-eyed glance, "since Dieppe."

It was a sharp blow. Whatever else he was, Chaucer was a professional and efficient. I had been running off with a schoolteacher in those days. He had met us on the boat going over. He and she had had a most satisfying talk about the year she had taken her diploma.

There was a change in Chaucer's conversation now we were at the bar. Academic research vanished. He was blatant.

"Interesting case, the Barclay case," he said. "Why did she do it?"

I headed him off. He was on at once to libel and slander. I headed him off again on to his holiday, but the taste for crime and law was growing fast in him. It was new interest suddenly born. They had passed, he said, the mill at Duffin, the scene of the Purdom murder.

"The farmer's wife who poisoned her husband," he explained. There was a don at Queens or somewhere who had been disqualified from driving. He had only once been to the law courts in his life, Chaucer said (and he gleamed with the intention of never kissing a case now) and that was to hear an appeal. The appellant was the member of the gang of safe-breakers.

"It just shows you what a small place the world is. The man sitting next to me in court knew the prisoner. 'Pal of mine. Pal of mine,' he kept saying." Chaucer was enjoying himself. He looked younger and younger with every crime he mentioned.

He had actually been sitting next to somebody else's oldest friend. Chaucer's son had joined us now and blurted out:

"I don't think that woman doctor will get off, do you?"

"The husband of your chemistry mistress is a Q.C., isn't he?" Chaucer asked proudly of his son. Chaucer's age dropped to the early thirties.

Chaucer insisted on seeing me off to the door of my car. I was obliged to drive off. I drove out of the town to the bridge over the river and looked at the mild evening water where one or two men were fishing. . . . I was waiting for the moment when Chaucer and his son would be safely at dinner before I returned.

In an hour I was in Sophia's room. She was lying in bed.

"Didn't you get my message?" she said.

"You can't ring me. No telephone," I said.

"Silly," she said. "Come for me in the morning, early."

"About eleven," I said, knowing her habits.

"Earlier," she said.

"Ten thirty," I laughed.

"No, ten," she said.

This was an old game of ours and it soothed me. I was restored.

"Ring me from the call box," she said. "I'll come down."

When I got back to the cottage and saw its white solitary walls in the August moonlight, I saw she had been playing with me. Up and downstairs to the telephone she would go, yes; but she had been too "low" to come here. One gets jealous of ridiculous things. She would do anything for a telephone. I had a bad night and to teach her I waited until eleven o'clock before I drove back those ten miles to the hotel.

The porter was standing outside his desk as if waiting for me.

"Mrs. Barclay," he sneered even before I asked him, "has gone. She went out at half past nine. There's a note for you."

I took the letter and went out into the street to read it. I was not going to allow the porter to gaze at my destruction from the whited sepulchre of his old age. I was back instantly. Sophia said she had by mistake picked up Chaucer's little red exercise book, the bible of his journey, the chart of his life, with her magazine, and had only found it this morning. She had gone after him with it.

"I'm death," she said.

The Chaucers had left by bus an hour earlier and no one knew where. On the wall of the office was the calendar. The figure 26 stood out large.

When I look back at this period of Sophia Barclay's life and of my own the fatal difference between us is clear. I had no unconscious mind; Sophia had no conscious mind. When I waited at the hotel for her to ring up or to come back, listening to the combustion of the summer traffic passing to the holiday mountains, I had leisure to go through her character inch by inch. It is a delusion that distance or waiting breed mystery and encourage desire. At the end of an hour there was little of Sophia's character left. I knew that when she returned I would start putting it together again and the knowledge made me laugh. I was laughing at Chaucer. Sophia had really brought off her most brilliant coup. To take away the planner's plan, to make away with the policy of the most insured man on earth—this was dazzling of her. I imagined the moment of discovery, the recriminations between father and son. Chaucer would be defeated. Without his book he would not know whether he was to eat a sandwich or have the hotel lunch anywhere. He would be faced by a waterfall when he had expected a castle. It would be anarchy. For the first time he would be out of touch. Unless—and I laughed even more when I imagined Sophia saying this to him as she certainly would—his unconscious had been at work. For what phenomenal motive, in obedience to what primitive force, had he left the twenty-sixth blank?

On that decisive morning in our lives Sophia was true to herself. She had as little idea of where she was as she had of the whereabouts of the Chaucers. Her inevitable telephone calls conveyed this. I damned his little red book. She called me intolerant.

"I must put this right. It's frightful of me. It is not as if they were friends," she said.

And the next call:

"Still no luck. They must have gone on to Snowdon."

"But that's a terribly long way. Come back."

"I can't wreck their holiday," she said.

"What about us?" I said. "Are you running off with me or with Chaucer *père et fils?*"

"Speaking French does not make it funny," she said. "People are serious," she added censoriously.

"Not Chaucer," I said.

"His wife is dead. He's a widower," she said.

The Snag

Like divorce, death brought out all Sophia's profound feeling for the respectable. I was made to feel outside the pale of the central glooms of life.

I found out where she was.

"I'm coming for you," I said.

"Two cars again. Don't be silly," she said. "I'm going to Snowdon."

"So am I, then," I said. "I can't wait wondering what all this chasing after widowers is about."

Her voice changed

"All what?" she said very coldly.

"This," I said.

I recognized as I drove after her that what I had just said was disastrously wrong. I recognize after five years that it was one of those unforgivable mistakes one makes in one's life. Sophia was always doing the wrong thing, but to call it "all this" was to make her feel in the right about it. I had once called the Barclay case "all this." I spent the rest of the journey trying not to see the ludicrous side of our situation; the Chaucers voyaging without chart, Sophia pursuing them without knowing where they were, and myself pursuing her, and all of us not meeting at the mountain sacred to Welsh tourism. I was wrong.

The first thing I saw at that point of the mountain were the light railway starts for the summit was Sophia's small green car. Near it stood Chaucer's son. Round-shouldered, thin, pale, glum, he was staring enviously at the heavy motor traffic on the road.

I got out of my car. "Where are you all?" I asked.

He watched a motorcycle go roaring by and out of

sight before he could collect himself to answer. He was deeply enjoying noise.

"Hullo," he said passively. "Dad's with Mrs. Barclay. They told me to wait here in case you came."

"Where are they?"

"Gone up," he said, nodding to the mountain. "Dad's taken her. We were in a mess. Dad couldn't find our book. She had taken it. We missed two buses."

He spoke in the relieved manner of one who was grateful that his father had missed something for once.

"If Mrs. Barclay hadn't found it and brought it we wouldn't have got here. She was very decent, she gave us a lift—that little Humber can shift when she steps on it."

But I was looking up the green slopes and hard shoulders of the mountain. I was listening for her chatter.

"You won't see them," he said.

"I'm sorry I've made you miss the trip. Why didn't you go?"

"Doesn't interest me," said the boy. "My idea was to take the motor bike to France. They didn't want me."

"How long have they gone?"

"I don't know. They're going right up to the top, though. When she gave us a lift that is what she said: 'Now we can all go right up to the top.' Dad and I were only going half-way. You see, she said she'd give us a lift on afterwards. She said she'd never been to the top of a mountain before in her life."

The boy was grinning, but he stopped shyly and frowned at me thoughtfully. Then he burst out:

"Do you think she got a fair deal in that case? She was

telling Dad about it, he knows the judge. He said she ought to have got a thousand pounds. That woman doctor has, in the paper this morning. Do you think the law's always right? I've never met anyone who's been in a case before. There was trouble about a water burst in Dad's office and Mother wanted him to bring a case, but he wouldn't, so we didn't get anything. I agree with Mrs. Barclay, you've got to go all out."

All out with Chaucer!

Many hours passed before they came down the mountain. Sophia was hot and blushed when she saw me. I had hardly ever seen her look so impudent. At half past six that evening I was following them all as she drove them a few miles on to their next stopping place and, as usual, she was soon out of sight. When I caught them up she had run into the bus from Llanberis. They spent the night of the twenty-sixth in hospital. It was the beginning of their courtship.

Chaucer never loses touch with old friends. After their marriage I had no sight of Sophia or Chaucer for a good five years. But then, one evening in London, when I was standing in a cinema queue trying to calm a girl I was with, who was making a scene, I heard the well-known voice drilling through the traffic noises of a London Saturday night: Chaucer. There was no escape. I dined with them. It was for them an elated dinner party. Thank heaven there were other guests.

No rattling electric trains near Chaucer's well-found house. No frantic decoration on its walls. There was not a touch of Sophia's in the place. From his previous marriage Chaucer has accumulated much of the larger mahogany and she had become larger to match it—larger, plump, and silently contented. He looked down the table at her with pride. There were university couples at dinner—not at all Sophia's set—but there was no talk of academic women. Chaucer gossiped as if he had been the second cousin of a peer. He was on to judges, courts, queer cases, points of law. At first I was amused; then I realized Chaucer was exhaustive. I became alarmed. Rightly. The great bores are men of mastery and nerve.

"That is how we got married," he was shouting to us all, pointing a hurrahing finger at her down the table. "She nearly killed me. Stole my papers, crashed into a bus, and the next thing I was at the altar. I could have brought a case. And there's an interesting point. The insurance company fought. There was a point of law. It's the only time my picture has been in the papers."

I saw it on her face. They were two blissful news items. Publicity, scandal, had been Chaucer's craving.

"Or mine," she said submissively.

"Oh, how can you say that!" protested Chaucer, with pride on her behalf. "The Barclay case, don't be shy, tell them about it."

"No, you," she said.

"It's your story—still, if you won't, I must."

"And don't forget the little red book," she said with a voluptuous wriggle.

I couldn't believe my ears. There was a pause in which they both glanced at me, she satisfied and fulfilled; he slyly and, what was worse, protectively. The glance conveyed that she was the scandal I could never have made the most of and I was the hole-in-corner despair from whom he had saved her. But for him she might now be having rows with me in cinema queues on Saturday nights.

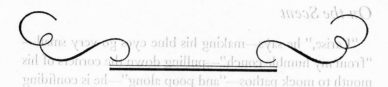

On the Scent

A big, oblong man, Manningtree gets out of bed in the morning, briskly, straightens up at once, yawns, blows out his chest, then puts on a violet silk dressing gown and is about to shout joyfully:

"Wakey, wakey! Rise and shine! Lash up and . . .."—but no! He looks across to the bed where his gnat of a wife is sleeping under a little fizz of dyed red hair, with her busy mouth wide open, even in sleep, and he stops. Putting on a stealthy look and lifting his knees high, he tiptoes out of the room. Manningtree's face is important. It has a quality that can only be called blatantly public, like a statue's; this is his fortune and his calamity. He is tall. He is handsome. At sixty-two, he still has beautifully polished fair hair, a pink, boyish skin, and still, blue eyes, and, at times, total calm. This is his fortunate side. His stealthy, dramatic look as he tiptoes out of the room is an aspect of the calamitous one; it empties clubs and bars, it empties sofas and corners of rooms at parties, it has emptied messes in two world wars. It is the look of the relentless, booming, whispering story-teller.

Take getting up in the morning.

"I arise," he says—making his blue eyes go very small—"from my humble couch"—pulling down the corners of his mouth to mock pathos—"and poop along"—he is confiding—"to the end of the passage"—he is now secretive—"to get in the milk and the papers." Then he makes a peculiar movement of his lower jaw, which shoots out sideways, at the same time almost closing his mouth, so that he speaks a little grindingly through his teeth and conveys a lurking, better-not-be-caught-red-handed impression. He continues in a tone now sordid, "to see what's going on in the world," and, at this, his face becomes handsome, nearly blank—"to see," he says disparagingly, "if there is anything of interest."

He stares at you when he says this for a long time and most people have to lower their eyes as one does after looking at the blind statue of some soldier or politician. And then the conspiring look comes on again; he leans towards you with his jaw shooting sideways, driving you bit by bit into your corner until you want to put up your hands and surrender, and he goes very mean and nasty about the mouth. "And pick up the post to see if the Manningtree millions have turned up," he adds.

So he describes the first half-hour of the day. His wife, who does not sleep well in spite of doctors and pills of all kinds, is awake, but keeps her eyes closed because she has seen and heard this performance every morning of her married life—except for the war—but she opens them when he brings in her breakfast, keen and singing.

"No luck, old girl! No Manningtree. Boo hoo hoo," he says, collapsing his face.

She could scream.

184

"Bunny's a fool, an ass, a dolt!" she tells her friends, and all her little bits of jewellery repeat the message in flashes from her neck, her ears, her fingers. "I think I shall go mad. We live in two pokey little rooms. I have nothing to put on. He hasn't even got a pension. Go to London! Go to Paris! My dear, we can't afford the bus fare to go to the cinema. That gas fire is the only comfort I've got in life." She lowers her voice to a dirty whisper. "As for you know what—we gave that up two years after we were married."

And then she tells them the story of this disastrous marriage. There she was, a woman with brains, attractive, too. Men with brains, she never could resist them: Angus, Charles, Duncan, Max—look what they have done. Angus an admiral, Max, governor of somewhere—but just because she was potty about a shifty and brilliant painter who jilted her for an Irish waitress, she had to go and marry Bunny Manningtree on the rebound. He worked for a travel agency and was hopeless at it.

"Of course," she says, pulling herself together, "he is a Manningtree. Lord Manningtree is his cousin. They are all bankers, shipbuilders, Cabinet ministers, worth millions."

"I always have a look at the *Times* to see if any of them have died," she says, twisting her little face, for she has caught something of his habits after twenty-five years— "but the fool! He even says he doesn't think he's any relation at all, won't even write a letter and here we stick in this hole. And I had talent! We scrape, we sit. I stay in bed half the day and he comes in the evening with his library book, and he reads bits out to me. History! Mexico! That's the latest thing. The Aztecs."

She gives a hysterical laugh.

185

"D'you know—I asked what he wanted to do when he was a boy. Do you know what he said? An Aztec priest!!!" She is wrong about this. After breakfast Manningtree walks across the park to earn, as he puts it, "the sordid daily crust." He has an excellent figure, he is presentably dressed, he has the serene, dummy-like expression that would delight any tailor. She is wrong about his wanting to be an Aztec; that was years ago, before the war. He has moved southward since then, across Panama, down the Andes. He is with the Incas, these days. After a few hundred yards, his face attracts attention from passers-by. It has begun to move. It is dramatizing certain arguments about the Virgins of the Sun. He is going over their chief temples, their convents set apart from the Inca towns. He arrives eventually at Macchu Picchu. One hundred female skeletons have been found at that Inca hide-out—were they Virgins of the Sun or were they Manco II's concubines or simply Indians who had fled with him from the Spaniards? Manningtree has doubts. He scents a mystery and his blue eyes go very small. The only way to clear it up is to go back to the sixteenth century. He does this. He has got out of Cuzco unobserved by the Spaniards and although he knows the Inca roads well, the stone causeways six feet wide, scratched on the sides of the Andes or choked by the jungle, he also knows that the only safe, secret way is to go by the Urabamba river. He sets off, with a machete—but back he has to come because the old, old question has arisen. How is he dressed? How is he disguised? At this word, the artfulness of his face is so blatant that children fifty yards away think he is going to eat them.

Alas, Manningtree has now to postpone the answer.

186

He has arrived. He straightens his face and goes into a door-way marked "Staff only," in the Hildegarde Memorial Museum.

This museum had been the white elephant of the city for two generations. The Council would have liked to have sold it or pulled it down; they could not do so. But fashions change. Once deserted except on rainy days, the museum is now visited by thousands of people every year.

It is a fantastic, cream-washed, Neo-Gothic mansion built about 1820 in the park—which was attached to it—by an Austrian archduke for his mistress, the twelfth Duchess of Taxminster. There is a Byron story about her. After the archduke died it was taken over, in the late 70's, by the intellectual son of the steel magnate Rudolf Dabchild and his crippled wife, Hildegarde von Hochfeld-Mannheim, who inherited the Kreutzer fortune. These two beetle-like creatures were compulsive, voracious, indiscriminate collectors. Trainloads, vanloads of remarkable furniture, armour, Spanish choir stalls, icons, Italian ceilings, porcelain, tapestries, pictures, weapons, costumes of all the ages, Chinese, Japanese, and Indian objects, archaeological relics, and the usual cases of Polynesian masks, canoes, poisoned arrows, and stuffed birds and so on, arrived at the mansion and choked it. When Dabchild's wife died, he unloaded it on the appalled city and called it the Hildegarde Memorial Museum. Fortunately a rich trust supported it. It was run by antiquarians originally, but lately, since the dissolution of the British Empire, people who would have been generals or governors of African and Indian provinces in earlier days now dominate the committee. One of these, remembering Manningtree's record in the war, got him his job. Or rather his wife did, by circulating the gossip that he was a connexion of the great Manningtrees.

Even now, Bunny Manningtree won't say what he was doing in the war. He simply says he was sitting on his bottom on the Shetlands, "pooped around" for a few months in the United States, and had something to do with one or two "wheezes." "No initiative," his wife says. "He let them push him into Supply." "Supplying wheezes," he explains. The word "wheeze" comes out with a lingering malicious glee as if he were a schoolboy who has just bought a trick glass of beer at a joke shop or written to another boy in invisible ink. All the same, bits of the war, he says, "had an interest." Up in the Shetlands, for example, he got friendly with the seals and collected moss.

Whatever it was, it was a dead end, as far as his peacetime prospects were concerned. He stands (it must be said that is one thing he can do: stand properly; few people can) about ten yards inside the main entrance of the Hildegarde, looking at the moons of his nails.

Once or twice a year an old acquaintance spots him.

"Good heavens—Manningtree? What are you doing here?"

"On the strength," says Manningtree calmly. And then his other face jostles the calm one away and he narrows his blue eyes, slips his lower jaw sideways, and says in a chewing, secretive, and sordid voice: "Actually—guide. I show the hoi polloi round. Coach parties. It's terrifying." Then his face changes and he straightens to mention the finer aspects of his job.

"V.I.P.'s, too. French mayors, Siamese ambassador, Russians."

He puts his hand to his mouth and coarsely whispers again:

"Minister of Labour last Tuesday."

"There are one or two things worth a look," he says. He leads his friends down the fantastic corridors, passing statues, Japanese paintings, Indian carvings, cases of porcelain. He comes to a door and a sly look comes on.

"Private apartments of the archduke," he says. The friends admire.

"Hoovered three times a week," he says to the ladies. He beckons them on to the centre piece. It is, of course, the canopied bed of the archduke.

"See the little secret staircase?" he says, nodding to a corner by the bed. He looks noble. His friends grin. He is disappointed by the blatancy of the universal reaction, especially if one of the men lags behind for a second look at the staircase and says: "Very convenient."

Manningtree's sinister face comes on, reprovingly. He nods to the staircase.

"That is why Bismark tore up the Treaty."

No one has any idea what he is talking about.

Afterwards as the party leaves, Manningtree shakes hands and they go off saying: "Poor old Bunny."

At five o'clock he collects a book or two from the library, goes home, and after dinner he reads. Suddenly he may say to his wife:

"Here's another so-called explorer repeating the same cock-eyed idea. No Inca in his senses would have built a fort there, where it could be dominated by any enemy outside. It wasn't a fort, it was a holy city. The rising sun strikes through the slit on the Intihuatana sundial."

189

No answer.

"Another howler," he says. "The saddle is not ten thousand feet up. I'd put it nearer eight thousand."

"Perhaps it's grown since you were there," his wife says.

One Monday—Mondays are usually quiet in the winter—a foreigner comes to the Hildegarde Museum. He is a tall, well-built German with clipped grey hair, cold, wide, grey eyes, straight-nosed, straight-lipped, easy in carriage. He buys a guidebook at the counter, walks past Manningtree, and sets off round the museum on his own. As he passes he leaves behind him a worldly smell of cigar, caraway, and some other smell—a scent. The scent disturbs Manningtree. It makes him feel cold. Having nothing to do, he strolls off from room to room, looking for a sunny window. Once or twice he sees the foreigner in the distance. Manningtree's nose twitches. He moves to another room.

"Got it," he says at last. "*Vol de nuit.*"

The foreigner can be seen distantly through three doorways. Manningtree dreams.

"Hun. Baron, I suppose. Baltic family. Query, born Lubeck. Staff officer in war. No, not staff officer. Heidelberg, Oxford. Berliner. Villa in Dahlem, pretty district. Take a bus from the Kurfürstendamm. Forget the number."

Manningtree moves on. There is more sun in the south of the building. He goes to his favourite room—ancient costumes. His mind travels.

In those days, he recapitulates, the Incas must have held the roads they scratched on the mountains and they certainly had fortified places. They once shelled the Spaniards in Cuzco with white-hot stones. (That, by the way, does not excuse the public rape of several hundred Virgins of the

Sun.) Anyone trying to get the gen on Macchu Picchu and to see what Manco II's boys are up to had better take to the jungle following the Urabamba through its gorges. Have to be fit, of course.

Manningtree takes to the jungle. He slips below the fortified line. He has jungle cunning. In the hot depths of the gorges he can keep alive on bananas. He finds a deserted hut and there at night he hangs his shirt over the entrance to keep out the night air of the Andes. After sixty miles on foot, swollen with bites, he is at the base of Macchu Picchu two thousand feet above him. Up he goes; as he gets nearer he sees a sight to shake the spirit of any man. Two bodies come hurtling through the air, pass over him, and crash into the gorge. Aha! The High Priest has caught a couple trying to get to the Virgins of the Sun. Manningtree pauses to consider the old, old problem. How is he dressed? Inca robes? But did the Incas wear Inca robes? Didn't the Spaniards make them wear Spanish costume? And what was Spanish costume in Extremadura in the sixteenth century? An idea comes to Manningtree, a wheeze. Suppose he appears in Macchu Picchu dressed as he is now, in a navy-blue suit with light chalk stripes, white collar, school tie? Why not? Take them by surprise, eh? Probably run away. That is exactly what happens. Men posted at the main gate make a bolt for it. He walks in and catches a boy—always ask a boy—*Donde está* the High Priest?—always make for a priest. Nasty sight here, by the way: two more men tied by their heels and hanging head down over the precipice—two more cases of trying to get to the Virgins of the Sun. A whole crowd of High Priests come along. They rush him. He is arrested at once. He is tried in the court house—

191

usual charge, Virgins of the Sun again; and, by the way, archaeologists are wrong: the courtyard described as residence of Manco II is actually *below* the residence. The military fellers get out their clubs and prepare to beat him to death and then pitch his body into the gorge.

A nasty fix this, but Manningtree has an answer to it. He worked that one out when he was settling the dress problem a few hours ago when he was climbing up the hill. Manningtree's face takes on one of its most public leers of profound cunning, visible (one would guess) but for the Andes, as far away as the Pacific Ocean.

"Oh, High Priest," Manningtree says. "Throttle down a moment. I've been having a peep at your sundial. Art thou not all het up about sunrise and sunset, and what-have-you? Time in short? Am I right? Splendid! well, let me put a little problem to you, something to think over. I come from the future. You're yesterday as far as I am concerned, I'm tomorrow. Tomorrow's sun has already risen before today's has set. D'you follow?"

One of the enclosed Virgins of the Sun stops weaving vicuna and looks out of a window and exclaims:

"Oh thou!"

The fellows put down their clubs and they start a pijaw nineteen to the dozen—not loudly, by the way. At that altitude, the air is thin and voices are soft, a curious point. Manningtree takes his opportunity and talks in signs to the Virgin of the Sun. Where does that road lead to? he signals. She replies, by signs. To the real secret city. Manningtree thought as much. He has always held that Macchu Picchu was an outpost, a decoy. He memorizes her information.

Never write anything down! He has always memorized everything.

The German visitor to the Hildegarde has come back to the room where Manningtree has been standing and has been watching him for several minutes. He has noticed that Manningtree is standing in front of a large glass case containing Spanish costumes and at first the German thinks Manningtree is talking to someone. Then he has the idea that since no one is visible the person must be hidden in the glass case. This does not startle him. He is alerted. He has recognized an interesting idea, a possible experience; it has, unfortunately, been used in films. He feels drawn to Manningtree and approaches him.

"Excuse me, sir," he says in rather stiff, good English, "are you by any chance the head director of the museum?"

Manningtree puts on his blank face at once.

"No I'm not, I'm sorry. Can I be of any help?"

"I wonder if you could direct me to the archaeological section?" says the German. "Are you an official?"

Manningtree's nose twitches. He has smelled *Vol de nuit* again. He has a strange cold feeling of being carried into the past.

"Oh no," says Manningtree. "I'm just a sort of chap keeping a sort of an eye." And, in fact, he opens one eye to significant wideness.

"I beg your pardon," says the German. "You are a visitor like myself."

"Oh no," says Manningtree. "For my sins this is where I earn the daily crust. Follow me. I'll show you."

193

On the Scent

The German stares at him; then he smiles. He remembers. He remembers what the English are like; very soon, as the textbooks say, Manningtree is likely to make a joke. The German prepares himself for this. They walk in a friendly fashion across the room together, and nodding to the cases, Manningtree says in his sinister voice: "This is where we keep the *disguises*."

"The disguises?" the German repeats politely. Somewhere here, at any moment, will come the joke.

"The costumes," says Manningtree with wonderful coolness.

"Ah!" The German is relieved. The joke has been accomplished. Manningtree becomes friendly.

"Have you seen the Private Apartments?"

"Yes. Of little interest," says the German. "Just the little incident of Bismark and the Treaty."

Manningtree is delighted. One does not often meet the man with inside knowledge. But he is still worried by the smell of *Vol de nuit*.

"Here," he says, "this is what you want. Archaeology. There are two rooms. Early British village?" Manningtree offers. "The Western lake culture?"

"Africa?" He hesitates shyly. "Inca?"

The German shrugs his shoulders and walks brusquely forward.

"This is what I want." He opens his catalogue. "The Mayas."

Vol de nuit! Maya! Manningtree suddenly knows something. His face closes. He had been right first go-off.

"You speak English very well. You were up at Oxford?" he asks.

194

"Yes. I had been at Heidelberg. My family comes from Lubeck, but I live in Berlin now."

"Dahlem," says Manningtree.

"Yes," says the German warmly.

"Lovely trees. You can get a bus, I seem to remember, from the Kurfürstendamm, I forget the number—was it eighty-six?"

"Interesting," says the startled German. "When were you there last?"

"Never," says Manningtree. "Not actually, ever."

"This is extraordinary," says the German.

Manningtree puts on his most asinine, blushing, apologizing face.

"Always interested in places, local buses, trains. I collected time tables at school. I used to play at running goods trains all over Europe—the world actually. Fun. Something of interest."

The German is puzzled and takes a long look at Manningtree. He is weighing up the question of madness, for Manningtree looks very childish, stupid, his chin dropping, his mouth open. Manningtree changes the subject.

"I'm not a Maya man," he says. "I'm afraid I'll be no good to you," Manningtree apologizes. "I moved on to the Incas."

"The Incas, now, that's another thing," he goes on. "I mean I'm not a scholar. I just potter. The priesthood, the roads. Clever people. Time, for example. They understood it."

The German edges away.

Manningtree follows him closer.

"And another thing—how they got the information through the Andes. Two thousand miles, three more like it. No writing, no letters, no telephone—memorized it." He pauses. "What was their secret?"

His face is blameless.

"No radio," he concludes.

The German gives a sharp turn of his head. He is uncertain. Is Manningtree mad? Manningtree is now studying the cases of Mayan objects.

"Mayas are interesting too. You know them well?" says Manningtree humbly.

"Yes," said the German.

"I tried it, before the war. There were too many problems," says Manningtree. "I moved out of Mexico on to the Incas. For instance, here's a thing, I bet you can tell me, the sort of detail that I get stuck in, I mean, fed up with. The palace at Mitla—you know the palace at Mitla? I mean the second Incan palace."

"But you *do* know the Mayas!" says the German suspiciously.

"Nothing," says Manningtree. "I mean the High Priest had put the wind up the kings and all that and the kings got very cunning."

Manningtree begins his well-known jaw-sliding and significant eye-rollings.

"They cut three back doors so that they could nip out fast before the old boy could spot them—rather neat? The snag is—and this is where I stick—if you go to Mitla today there are no back doors. And, what's more, if you look up your Father Bourgoa you'll see he says there were six rooms. Actually there are only four. What d'you make of that?"

"Bourgoa's sources were unreliable," says the German affably. "He was repeating hearsay. What year were you there?"

"Alas and lackaday, never," says Manningtree. "Never had the wherewithal. I just go pooping around old books."

"Pooping!" exclaims the German.

"Just pooping and pottering," says Manningtree.

" 'Pooping'—I don't understand that English word," says the German. "I have heard it . . . yes . . ."

The German, who up to now has had simply a sharp, intelligent German face, like thousands of others one sees along the Baltic, suddenly has a memory and *his* face changes. He seems to put on weight as if he had just eaten too much. His cheeks swell over his jaw, which fattens; tears like juices come into his eyes, which nearly close and look sly. At the sight of this, Manningtree's pink face blushes, his eyes begin watering too. He also fattens. The two men stand melting in front of each other like blushing snowmen as though the temperature of the room has shot up twenty degrees.

"I envy you going to Mexico," says Manningtree.

"Oh I haven't been there either," says the German.

The German goes on and, for the first time, his English syntax is clumsy:

"But it is always historical that makes for you the interest? I don't think so. When we met on the night train from New York to Chicago in December 1940, was that pooping, Captain Manningtree? You were interested in the Virgins of the Sun."

Manningtree stares at him.

197

"I was a pooper, too!" exclaims the German with delight, extending his hand. "Hochstadt."

"Hochstadt!" Manningtree nods. And then he winks at the German.

"*Vol de nuit*, a great mistake, old boy. Terrible giveaway. We followed you all over the States. It clings. No offence. What are you up to now?"

The German looks humble.

"I have a small cinema," he says sadly. "Not Dahlem any more."

"Hoi polloi, eh? Well, I suppose," says Manningtree," it brings in the daily crust."

And, in sympathy, he looks over the floors, walls, and ceilings of the Hildegarde Memorial Museum with disgust.

"By the way, I always wondered," says Manningtree, "how did you manage after we got your radio?"

"Like the Incas," says the German. He has got his revenge. He has made a joke.

The Hildegarde Museum closes. Manningtree walks home across the park. He tells his wife about the encounter.

"I recognized him the moment he came in," he says. "Smelt him. I didn't let on. I didn't say anything. 'Aha!' I thought. 'Baron von Trondheim,' I says to meself! I just lay low"—he crouches. "I shammed dead"—he closes his eyes. "Memory got busy. He recognized me too. I don't know how, deep fellow."

"I wonder!" says his wife.

"Ah," says Manningtree, screwing up one eye and rubbing a finger joint on a thoughtful tooth. "Still an agent, I think. He gave the name Hochstadt."

Manningtree's pleasure fades. He looks gloomy.

"Manningtree millions not arrived, I suppose? No. Ah well. Have to wait for another war, but I'll be past it. My memory's going. I couldn't remember the number of the Dahlem bus. Bad show."

Citizen

I wonder if you go to picture exhibitions and if you saw the drawings at the W Gallery a month or so ago. Italian drawings, by a woman—Effie Alldraxen. Very good notices, the critics gave her. Very gratifying to me. She is my daughter. There was one large drawing that several of our friends mentioned—typically Italian, the picture of one of those *palazzo* courtyards in Rome with a statue in it. It was one she called *The Father*. She caught the feeling that you have in Rome, of statues being everywhere—stone people (do you know?) threatening, appealing, almost walking about, crowding in, pushing the living off the pavement. One of the critics said she made the figure live—a curious statement, I thought, because stone and bronze are dead, aren't they? Of course, I don't know anything about art. I'm just a layman, a doctor. My business is illness. What interested me when I went to look at Effie's show was that the child was ill when she was doing the best of that stuff. I say "child"—a father's slip of the tongue; she is turned forty.

I hope not to sound harsh, but Effie has not been an easy child. I would describe myself as detached. I see so many sick people. She has been sending us telegrams all her life, and

before I opened the one she sent from Rome, where she was
doing that picture, I thought: "Now what mess has she got
into?" Effie's telegrams read as though she is doing her face
in the mirror—a dab here, a dab there, but with words. It
went: "In hospital, motor accident. No bones, not serious,
don't worry, just bad breakdown. Can you come immediately, not to bother, please if possible. Very well."

Children tear at one's bowels. In eight hours I was out of
the London rain and sitting by Effie's bedside in Rome, listening to her childish voice. She had not been in a motor accident. She had been pushed by the bumper of a slow-mov-
ing car in the Corso and had been knocked down by a
bicycle.

"I think—" she said after we had gone over the incident
several times. "I think," she said, stubbornly putting up her
chin, "I must have been trying not to get married."

Effie is a small woman, and although she is growing
plump, she looks younger than she is. She will be forty-one
next June. She was sitting up in bed, and she had the pleased,
shining, new, ashamed look, rather wet and cunning, of a
golden spaniel that has been dressed up in shawls by children and is presently going to make a bolt for it into the
garden.

"To Mr. Wilkins," she said.

"And who is he?" I asked.

"He was on the train when you saw me off from London.
Schoolmaster," she said. For testing one out, she has a small,
high, plaintive voice.

"I don't remember him," I said. "But what's the matter?
Is he married already?" One of the difficulties of Effie's
life has been her love of other women's husbands.

"Oh, no!" said Effie, giving a squeal of pleasure. She loved this kind of conversation. "He hasn't got a wife." Then she looked at me slyly. Effie is proud of her turbulent history. "I suppose his not being married is the trouble," she said.

Effie has two voices and two kinds of laughter. Her usual voice is small and sweet—the matter-of-fact voice of a girl of five—and she uses it for things that are true. The laughter that goes with it is the high squeal that used to enchant us when she was little. This voice is, no doubt, too arch for a woman of her age. Her other voice is dry, abrupt, grown-up, bold, and mannish, and it drops to short, doggish barks of laughter. In this voice, Effie does not often tell the truth. I knew now that Effie was going to tell me a lie next, because she arranged her bedclothes and looked me gruffly in the eye.

"You are going to be cross with me," she said, in the brisk manner. "I've started doing it again."

"What?"

"Making happenings," she said. She blushed.

I did not answer.

"I'm being followed," said Effie.

"By Mr. Wilkins?" I said, guessing.

"Oh, no, no," she barked.

"By some Italian?" I said.

Effie was so startled that she stopped laughing. I could see that I had put an idea into her head, perhaps for use in the future. There is something innocent about her. She had been a fortnight in Italy and it had not occurred to her that an Italian might follow her in the street, though she knew they followed other women. She had not thought of this because it was she who, in her day-dreams, was always the follower.

"Oh, no," she said. "Not a man." And then she added primly, correcting me: "Not followed. Accompanied."

After a moment, she went on. "Everywhere," she said. "In the street. I have to make room. I have to step out of the way. That's how I got knocked down. There wasn't room."

Effie stared at my stare. "I can't see whether you're looking at me, Daddy," she said. "The light is on your glasses."

"But who accompanies you?" I said.

"Oh, I knew you'd understand! Give me my drawings from the table," she said. "I'll show you. No, all of them. Not this one. Not this—flowers, rather nice, don't you think? Here it is. This one." She pointed. "It comes with me."

There was simply a drawing of the courtyard of a Roman palace, but there was no one in it.

"The statue," she said. "It walks with me everywhere I go." There was certainly a statue in the foreground of the drawing. She broke into real tears. "Silly?" she sniffed. "It came . . . here . . . this morning. But it's gone, now you're here. Not a fool—I, not you. I mean me—I'm not. It's true." And then she said, with a touch of aesthetic shame: "It's bronze, very late, 1884."

I suppose I owe my great influence with my daughter to the fact that I have made it an absolute rule to believe everything she says. I have never known her to be unpractical. She is brisk and domestic—a drawer-tidier, a sock-darner, a saucepan-buyer (one would say)—and she is pretty. Her fair hair is duller than it used to be, and she has eyes the colour of dark ginger. A poet might call them "orbs." She dresses oddly, as spinsters do, but that is because her practical instinct makes her do a little something different with everything. She was now doing something with a statue.

"It must make a terrible noise," I said.

"Frightful," she said. "And such a bad period."

The effect that Italy has upon Anglo-Saxons is always impressive. In a couple of days, when Effie's temperature was down, I went to look at her persecutor. The *palazzo* is on the street that leads to the bridge you cross to get to Sant' Angelo. There is a wide entrance smelling of cold candle smoke, and then one walks between double rows of columns into the courtyard beyond, where the colonnade continues on three sides of the building. On the fourth is the higher brick wall of some large house, relieved by creepers and fountains. After the hot street, this courtyard is cool and enchanting. Which of the figures had Effie's wanton mind chosen? I looked at them. The statues were set off in arches or placed among shrubs. They stood amid the dark gloss of creepers and beside fountains. The chief fountain was against the back wall, where three Tritons, the mask of disaster upon their spreading mouths, spouted into the tank beneath them; in the corners of the court two other pipes of water spoke out in higher voice beneath the hanging foliage. The air was as still and cool and golden as white wine; the place was filled with the sounds of water notes, high and low, like faraway talk and quiet laughing. One could fancy that this sound was the classical jargon of the figures standing near or posed under the twenty arches of the colonnade. Apollo, conceited in cheek and buttocks

204

—was it he Effie had chosen? Or Mercury, off on one of his record flights? The Venus, vacant-minded, or that careerist Diana? Which of all those white, finger-pointing gods and goddesses, those stooping nymphs and skilful boys, with their grubby, blind eyes and stone-deaf ears? As I entered the courtyard, my steps seemed to have frozen the movements of immortals, who, once my back was turned, would resume their irreconcilable and impossible lives.

I come out of this disturbing episode in the life of my family so much better than anyone else that I have no reluctance now about describing the large bronze statue that was obviously Effie's. It stood on a high plinth in the middle of the courtyard. Bronze. More than life-size, it was the naked figure of a man; on the pedestal were boldly cut out a name and, beneath it, the words *"Cittadino Esemplare"* —"The Exemplary Citizen." He was a man in the prime of life—a merchant, a burgher, a city father of some kind. His features were strong, his body muscular, boldly veined, broad-chested, overbearing. The legs were powerful; the expression of the face tragic, jealous, authoritative, unreasonable, and morose. The large hands were the open hands of a maker—a breadwinner's hands, which could stun an enemy or drive a woman. The Citizen was the not-to-be-questioned head of a large family (one would guess), a master of the marriage bed, the married man in absolute degree.

Mr. Wilkins came with me on this visit to the courtyard —the Mr. Wilkins Effie had spoken of when I got to the hospital, and whom I had made it my business to get in touch with. I glanced at Mr. Wilkins. I stared again at the statue. What a rival!

I must describe Mr. Wilkins. If my portrait appears to be unfavourable, it is because Mr. Wilkins was one of those men who enter enthusiastically into the art of making an unfavourable impression. He was a tall man, fortyish, with dry hair, wearing a light-grey suit and a school tie. He had a difficulty with the letter "i." We first met in the bar of my hotel to drink what he called "a glass of wain."

"Ai run a school," he said. He bent down and up from his thin waist as he talked—a habit picked up from talking to little boys—keeping his hands fidgeting frivolously in his pockets as he did so. A friendly man, fizzing with descriptive talk, he was always in steadily rising spirits, but before he reached his limit, something checked him, his throat gave a click, and tears of apology came into his eyes. Unfairly, this suggested the shadiness of a double life.

I would have known him from Effie's account of him; she is a cruel mimic. He had been on the train when it left London, and on the motor coach from Paris across the Alps. They were in sight of Turin, she said, when Wilkins, who was sitting behind her, put his hand round the side of the high seat and tapped her on the shoulder. "Castle," said Wilkins. There are often white chapels on the tops of the steep hills of the lower Alpine valleys.

Effie bent forward to look up. "Shrine, I think," said Effie, who was working on her guidebook.

"Bai Jove!" said Wilkins. "You're raight, shraine."

A little later there was another tap. Then another. From Turin to Milan, and then on to Bologna and Florence, she said, Mr. Wilkins must have tapped away at her shoulder dozens of times. First she had to twist her neck towards him

as he put his face round the side of the seat; then she had to
turn her back and twist forward, craning to see what he was
talking about; after that she had to twist back towards him
to make a comment. She would see a head of dry hair, and
the head would be zigzagging, nose down, towards her,
behind a ragged moustache. Her replies were usually cor-
rections, for, in an educated way, Mr. Wilkins was often
mildly wrong in his information. In moments of rest, she
would hear him making a sishing noise behind her. He made
this sound, she discovered later, by rubbing his hands up
and down the thighs of his trousers, like a boy who is just
about to be caned. After Florence, her neck was stiff and
her right shoulder was hunched inward at an uncomfortable
angle from her efforts to avoid Mr. Wilkins's tap. In her
hotel, when she undressed, she looked on her delicate skin
for the mark.

I understood Wilkins at once. His distortion of the letter
"i" was not due to affectation. It sounded like a family
piety, a deference to a dear, dead, cultured sister; or it may
have been due to catarrh, for he spoke like a person holding
an inhaler to one nostril in order to keep on terms with a
distant cold. A woman can conceal her life, but Wilkins
could not hide his out-of-date appearance, his overfriendly
guiltiness. In his one-sided way, he had an air, but pinned to
his back there seemed to hang a notice that Effie must have
read at once: "Frantically desires some woman to pull him
together."

From shoulder-tapping, Effie said, Wilkins moved to a
feeble squeezing of the upper arm. Effie likes a strong hand.
In Milan, the party they were travelling with went to the

opera, and Wilkins slept through the first act, making a personal sound, with his free nostril, that was just above the note of the violins.

"Ai feah," Wilkins apologized to Effie, "Ai overdid the wain at luncheon."

They went to the cathedral in Milan. "Ai adore baroque," said Wilkins.

"Gothic," Effie said sharply.

"Mai word, Miss Alldraxen," Wilkins said with appetite, "Ai love it when you are severe. You're taking me in hand."

Before Leonardo da Vinci in Bologna it was: "Now you're going to put me through it." And in Rome, to the party at large as they sat at luncheon, Wilkins announced: "Bai Jove, Miss Alldraxen gave me some punishment in the Vatican this morning. It is what Ai need."

The actual proposal of marriage was made, Effie said, in the Colosseum at night. The floodlighting there penetrates the upper arches and turns the high brick colander into a place of strong-smelling shadows. There is a hoarse whispering of voices from invisible tourists. Across the brown darkness came the nasal syllables of guides.

"Torn—er—to pieces—er—by wild—er—animalls," a guide was saying as Wilkins took Effie's hand.

Effie said: "Don't be stupid," and got back, in a temper, to the motor coach, which was hooting for them. She has told me that the moment Wilkins declared himself, a sharp pain went into her shoulder and stayed there like a nail. It was, so to say, his last tap, and he had driven it home. She was annoyed as she took her seat in the coach, and then the annoyance went. I can see her looking with pride at the women of the party, who were already gossiping about

Mr. Wilkins and herself. "My rheumatism," her expression would signal to them. "I knew it would come."

I have seen Effie in love a great many times. I do not mean that she was now in love, but she was—as she likes to be—adjacent to love. When this happens, her nature changes; she even changes shape. Her bosom rises, her back straightens, she puffs out softly. Her voice becomes sad and wise, and has a peculiar soft hoot, a flute-like sound. Glumly, her head is raised. She feels she has the weight of the air before a thunderstorm upon her, the oppression that makes people complain of their heads, retire to a darkened room, and sicken. For to Effie love is illness. The sacred illness. Attentive doctors and pained nurses gather about an imaginary bed, which is not the bed of ecstasy but the bed of some satisfying ailment.

I will skip the passions of her childhood, but there was Mr. Lucas at the art school when she was eighteen. Mr. Lucas's wife would not divorce him; Effie became ill with a strained heart. Then there was a man called Bobby, who said: "It was only a passade." Effie with a year's neuralgia. Sinclair, wife and three: bronchitis. Allardyce, Roman Catholic, judicial separation: migraines. Macdonald, wife in India: imaginary pregnancy. I could go on. If there was an unmarriageable man in love with someone else, Effie's hospital instinct would find him at once. If an unmarried man fell in love with her, as Wilkins did, she bit his head off.

Effie knows all this very well. I had it out with her six or seven years ago—once and for all, as I thought—after she had sat for three days with a packed suitcase containing towels, sheets, and dish cloths on the stairs outside the studio of a painter called Gotloff, whom she planned to

move in on, but who had gone off in time to Paris. I found
her in hospital recovering from what she pretended was an
attempt at suicide. I shall not forget the long, promiscuous
smile on her face and the bark of satisfied laughter she gave
as I went to her bedside. "It is really marriage I am in love
with, not men," she said then.

So Effie was well equipped for the Wilkins affair. At
luncheon on the day after Wilkins had proposed, she was
telling the party about "my old pain"—the pain in her
shoulder. The women were soon offering her remedies.
After each suggestion, the pain would change its nature. It
shot from shoulder to head, from head to stomach, from
stomach to knees. Was it the food? Was it the wine? Was it
the water? Was it the Tiber, or Roman fever, or the drains?
The women gave orders to Wilkins, who went out to the
pharmacy and came back with a collection of medicines—
poultices, headache pills, throat pastilles, indigestion tablets,
liver pills, drugs, purges, and tonics. Also a kilo of cotton
wool—his own idea. The party went to the catacombs in
the afternoon, and Effie and Wilkins stayed behind at the
hotel. "No thermometer!" she said. Out Wilkins went again.
When he got back, Effie said, she was alone in the lounge.
"I am dying of thirst," she said. "Is there any mineral
water?"

Hearing a precise request, Wilkins was impelled to go it
one better. He sent for a brandy. When it was brought, he
sat beside Effie, with his hands on his long thighs, regarding
her with enthusiasm; illness in women was a form of surrender. In actual fact, of course, *he* was surrendering. In her
bounteous complaints, Effie was giving him something to
surrender to. He saw—I have no doubt—a house, a lifetime

marked by journeys up and downstairs to the body of the holy object, with trays and bottles. He may even have imagined the spit of temper and reprimand.

The brandy improved Effie; its subtle medicinal evocation of the beauty of past illnesses must have warmed her. She looked at Mr. Wilkins, who was waiting for more punishment.

"I suddenly saw," she said to me, "that he really meant it. I mean, he really did want to marry me." He was, to all appearances, what she had been looking for all her life since the age of three—a husband. They sat in the lounge on a deep, hot sofa. Holding her glass, leaning her head back and looking at the ceiling, she talked. Out of imitative sympathy, aroused by his love, Wilkins leaned back and looked at the ceiling also. They exchanged untrue versions of their own early lives. Mr. Wilkins stopped looking at the ceiling and gazed at Effie with headlong admiration.

"Bai Jove!" he exclaimed. "Ai have never had a past."

It was not a boast; it was not a confession. It was said in the dashing and reckless manner of one who, as far as pasts were concerned, was agog to spend the future living in hers. I am pretty certain that until this sentence of his Effie had no interest at all in Mr. Wilkins; the unlucky man had been damned in her eyes by his marriageable condition. But now he had revealed a difficulty; he was too utterly marriageable, and difficulty was indispensable to her.

I listened to Effie as she sat up in bed telling her story in her evasive, upside-down way. Her wet handkerchief was screwed up in one hand. She was laughing one minute and dabbing her eyes the next, while the nun kept coming into the room at the wrong moment and the Italian cars changed gears on the hill outside. She told me that Mr. Wilkins's words had made her compare their two cases. She must have paused to consider whether to re-edit her life story and to appear no longer in the role of the victim of other people's marriages but as an innocent waiting, neatly and circumspectly, for "love to come" at last. Effie was as good as any woman at altering the play she was acting in. I don't know—she didn't tell me this—but I don't mind betting that Effie replied: "I haven't had a real past, either."

But I wasn't there to speculate, so I asked her: "Yes, but what did you say to him? Did you tell him you would marry him?"

"Oh, no!" She squealed with the pleasure of maddening me. "You are funny. I told him I would have to think."

Everyone who has heard Effie say the word "think" agrees it has a musical sound that takes all suggestion of the process called "thought" out of it. To see her "thinking" is delightful. She looks as though she is listening to a voice singing on a distant mountain. But she is practical. Oh, always practical. She went off into the streets of Rome with her sketchbook, looking for something—some person, some place on which to drape her thoughts. She found the *palazzo* and its courtyard. Why did she choose the courtyard?

"It was so quiet, so expectant," she said to me.

Yes, I thought, and it had an obvious difficulty and flaw— The Exemplary Citizen. There was something terribly wrong about *Cittadino Esemplare*, 1884. He was an aesthetic mistake—the wrong period, on the wrong scale. Wherever one stood, that gloomy, dictatorial male rose like an implacable obstacle.

She sat down to draw. "I had a really big think," she said. "About Mr. Wilkins, about me—about everything." As her pencil worked, her mind undoubtedly set off on a number of short trips into Wilkins's future life. She was in Warwickshire, the headmaster's wife; she was wearing a new sage-green tweed, with a yellow scarf, unmistakably smarter than the wives of the masters. She saw her shoes—red, I expect, to make people talk. At the school, she introduced progressive ideas—mixed-coloured sweaters for the boys, perhaps a French afternoon in her drawing room, more Creative Art. There was a master—young, satanic, modern languages, shadows under his eyes, unhappy with a wife not quite his class. He avoided Effie at first. She said: "Why do you avoid me?" Frankly, he looked as though he would kill her, and then suddenly "it all came out." They watched football matches while he told her, under his breath, things that (she told him) he ought not to say. Difficult. She looked at his dark palm; the lines of two major love affairs were deeply cut under the little finger.

She shifted her thoughts to the matrons. One of them had to go—one whose nose was out of joint. The woman had obviously been in love with Mr. Wilkins for years, and, besides, where did the sherry go? There was also a sad one who made a hysterical scene about the school secretary and "poured out her heart" into Effie's lap. Effie was also getting to know the Christian names of the boys, tiptoeing in to give a pat to a pillow of a new boy who was crying. One who stole she saved, by timely psychiatry, from kleptomania.

It was twelve o'clock in the *palazzo* courtyard, Effie told me. She had heard the midday siren of some factory. The morning had passed quickly, and art is exhausting. She had been sitting on a stone step, and she was stiff. She got up and looked at the enormous statue from a new angle and then at her drawing. It was wrong. It was awful. Apart from anything else, the feet were wrong. She had not made them stand squarely on the plinth; the figure was half in the air. I have no doubt she was giddy with hunger, but she felt, she said, that she was going to cave in with a sense of incompetence and failure. She walked to the plinth and looked at the Citizen's feet, and saw the sculptor had easily succeeded where she had failed.

"Damn! I can't even draw now! I shall have to marry him!" she said aloud, in an irritable and snapping voice.

She must have spoken louder than she knew, for she was startled to hear the walls of the courtyard echo her words. Among those statues, she had the impression of being overheard. She was even more startled to feel one of those well-known taps on her shoulder. She was horrified. Mr. Wilkins! He had followed her! He had heard!

"I was so ashamed I couldn't move," Effie said. "I mean I really couldn't move. I was fixed to the spot. He was holding me. He was hurting. I could hardly turn my head, and when I did, I saw—"

Effie began to cry again. I think *I* had better describe what she says she saw. The hand on her shoulder was not the familiar hand of the schoolmaster. It was not a pink and playful human hand. It was far too large. The fingers were of metal, glossy and greenish-black; the back of the hand was black, polished, and had bold, sculptured veins. It was the hand of the Citizen. And at once, leaning half his weight on her, he got clumsily down from his plinth, with a clang loud enough to bring all that part of Rome to its windows. Moving his hand to her neck, he gave her a shove forward and, without pause, marched her stumbling out of the courtyard and onto the pavement, naked and twice life-size as he was, clang, clang, clang, through half a mile of street, he made for the hotel. It was lunchtime. The crowds on the pavement and street corners were thick, the sunlight was blinding and sickening, but the exemplary male barged on. Effie had to step out into the street to save herself from being trodden on by him. She collided with people. And they, the whole lunchtime crowd, treated the thing in the traditional manner of the Italian nation: they stared at the woman, not at the man. At last the Citizen got her to the Corso, and made to cross over to the Galleria, where—and how she dreaded it!—Mr. Wilkins was to be waiting. The traffic was heavy and fast, but the Citizen, that ungovernable married man, marched deafeningly across, now pushing his way ahead. He hauled her into the middle of the street, right in front of a car, and trod clean through a bicycle— a father not to be obstructed.

"But Mr. Wilkins—didn't he help? Didn't he see? What did he do?" I asked.

Mr. Wilkins did not have a chance. Nor did the police, the crowd, or the ambulance men. The statue even got into the ambulance when she was picked up.

"No one could stop him," Effie sobbed. "He came to the hospital. He came to this room. He was here all the time. He wouldn't let Mr. Wilkins in."

Effie stopped crying and lowered her eyes demurely. "He told me—Mr. Wilkins," she said, "that I'd overdone the wine."

She raised her eyes again. Even Effie must have seen that
she had gone too far. She quickly put out her hand and took
mine.

"I'm sorry, Daddy dear," she said. "He's gone. It's over.
You came, and he went."

The Key to My Heart

When Father dropped dead and Mother and I were left to run the business on our own, I was twenty-four years old. It was the principal bakery in our town, a good little business, and Father had built it up from nothing. Father used to wink at me when Mother talked about their "first wedding." "How many times have you been married? Who was it that time?" he used to say to her. She was speaking of the time they first ventured out of the bakery into catering for weddings and local dances. For a long time, when I was a child, we lived over the shop; then Mother made Father take a house down the street. Later still, we opened a café next door but two to the shop, and our idea was to buy up the two little places in between. But something went wrong in the last years of Father's life. Working at night in the heat and getting up at the wrong time of day disorganized him. And then the weddings were his downfall. There is always champagne left over at weddings, and Father got to like it and live on it. And then brandy followed. When Mr. Pickering, the solicitor, went into the will and the accounts, there was muddle everywhere, and bills we had never heard of came in.

The Key to My Heart

"Father kept it all in his head," Mother said, very proud of him for that. Mr. Pickering and I had to sort it all out, and one of the things we discovered was that what we owed was nothing to what people owed us. Mother used to serve in the shop and do the books. She did it, we used to say, for the sake of the gossip—to day-dream about why the schoolmistress ordered crumpets only on Thursdays, or guessing, if someone ordered more of this kind of cake or that, who was going to eat it with them. She was generally right, and she knew more about what was going on in the town than anyone else. As long as the daily and weekly customers paid their books, she didn't bother; she hated sending bills, and she was more pleased than upset when Mr. Pickering told her there was a good six hundred pounds owing by people who either hadn't been asked to pay or who were simply not troubling themselves. In a small business, this was a lot of money. It was the rich and the big pots in the country who were the worst of these debtors. Dad and Mother never minded being owed by the rich. They had both grown up in the days when you were afraid of offending people, and to hear my mother talk you would have thought that by asking the well-off to fork out you were going to kill the goose that lays the golden egg, knock the bottom out of society, and let a Labour government in.

"Think of what they have to pay in taxes," she would say, pitying them. "And the death duties!" And when I did what Mr. Pickering said, and sent out accounts to these people, saying politely that it had no doubt been overlooked, Mother looked mournful and said getting a commission in the army had turned my head. The money came in, of course. When Colonel Williams paid up and didn't dispute

it, Mother looked at his cheque as if it were an insult from
the old gentleman and, in fact, "lost" it in her apron pocket
for a week. Lady Littlebank complained, but she paid all the
same. A few did not answer, but when I called at their
houses they paid at once. But the look on Mother's face
was as much as to say I was a son ruining her life-work
and destroying her chances of holding her head up in
society. At the end of two or three months, there was only
one large account outstanding—a Mrs. Brackett's. Mrs.
Brackett did not answer, and you can guess Mother made
the most of this. Mother spoke highly of Mrs. Brackett, said
she was "such a lady, came of a wonderful family," and
once even praised her clothes. She was the richest woman in
the county, and young. She became my mother's ideal.

Mrs. Brackett was married to a pilot and racing motorist
known in the town as Noisy Brackett; it was she, as my
mother said, nodding her head up and down, who "had the
money." Noisy was given a couple of cars and his pocket
money, but, having done that, Mrs. Brackett paid as little as
she could, as slowly as she could, to everyone else. When I
talked about her account to other shopkeepers in the town,
they put on their glasses, had a look at their books, sniffed,
and said nothing. Every shopkeeper, my father used to say,
woke up in the early hours of the morning thinking of how
much she owed him, and dreaming of her fortune. You can
work out how long her bill with us had run on when I say it
was nearly two hundred and thirty pounds. The exact sum
was two hundred and twenty-eight pounds, fourteen and
fourpence. I shall always remember it.

The first time I made out Mrs. Brackett's bill, I gave it to
Noisy. He often came into the café to flirt with the girls, or

to our shop to see Mother and get her to cash cheques for him. He was a thin little man, straight as a stick and looked as brittle, and covered (they said) with scars and wounds from his crashes. He had the curly, shining black hair of a sick gypsy, and the lines of a charmer all over his face. His smiles quickly ended in a sudden, stern twitching of his left cheek and eye, like the crack of a whip, which delighted the women. He was a dandy, and from Mother he had the highest praise she could give to any man. He was, she said, "snobby."

When I gave Noisy our bill, he handed it back to me at once. "Be a sweetie-pie," he said, "and keep it under your hat until the day after tomorrow. Tomorrow's my payday, and I don't want the Fairy Queen to get her mind taken off it—d'you follow? Good! Fine! Splendid fellow! Bang on!" And, with a twitch, he was back in his long white Bentley. "Bring it yourself," he said, looking me up and down. I am a very tall man, and little Noisy had a long way to look. "It'll do the trick."

Noisy did not hide his dependence on his wife. Everyone except the local gentry liked him.

So on the Thursday, when the shop was closed and I could leave the café to the waitresses—a good pair of girls, and Rosie, the dark one, very pretty—I took the station wagon and drove up to Heading Mount, four miles out of the town. It was June; they were getting the hay in. The land in the valley fetches its price; you wouldn't believe it if I told you what a farm fetches there. Higher up, the land is poor, where the oak woods begin, and all that stretch used to belong to old Mr. Lucas, Mrs. Brackett's father, who had made a fortune out of machine tools. The estate was broken up when he died. I came out of the oak woods and turned into the drive, which winds between low stone walls and tall rhododendron bushes, so that it is like a damp, dark, sunken lane, and very narrow. Couples often walked up on Sundays in June to see the show of rhododendrons on the slopes at Heading; the bushes were in flower as I drove by. I was speeding to the sharp turn at the end of the drive, before you come to the house, when I had to brake suddenly. Mrs. Brackett's grey Bentley was drawn broadside across it, blocking the drive completely. I ought to have seen this was a bad omen.

To leave a car like that, anywhere, was typical of Mrs. Brackett. If there was a traffic jam in the town, or if someone couldn't get into the market, nine times out of ten Mrs. Brackett's car was the cause. She just stepped out of it wherever it was, as if she were dropping her coat off for someone else to pick up. The police did nothing. As she got back in, she would smile at them, raise one eyebrow, wag her hips, and let them see as much of her legs as she thought fit for the hour of the day, and drive off with a small wave of her hand that made them swell with apologies and blow up someone else. Sometimes she went green with a rage that was terrifying coming from so small a person.

Now, in her driveway, I left my wagon and walked round her car towards the house. It was an old L-shaped house, sheltered by sycamores and built in the grey flaking stone of our part of the country. They say her father paid only twelve thousand pounds for it, and that included two or three cottages and farm buildings. The kitchens and servants' rooms and garages were at one side of the L— modern buildings, screened by laurels. Not that there were often any servants there. There was a small circle of lawn in the front of the house, with a statue in the middle of it.

As I walked across the lawn, I realized I had missed the back lane to the house, and that I ought to have driven along a wire-fenced road across the fields to the farm and the kitchen, where the housekeeper lived. But I had not been up there for several years, and had forgotten it. As I walked towards the white front door, I kicked a woman's shoe—a shoe for a very small foot. I picked it up. I was a few yards from the door when Mrs. Brackett marched out, stopped on the steps, and then, as sharp as a sergeant, shouted: "Jimmy!" She was looking up at the sky, as though she expected to bring her husband down out of it.

She was barefooted, wearing a blue-and-white-checked shirt and dusty jeans, and her short, fair hair untidy, and she was making an ugly mouth, like a boy's, on her pretty face. I was holding out the shoe as I went forward. There was no answer to her shout. Then she saw me and stared at the shoe.

"Who are you? What are you doing with that?" she asked. "Put it down."

But before I could answer, from the other side of the buildings there was the sound of a car starting and driving off on the back road. Mrs. Brackett heard this. She turned and marched into the house again, but in a few seconds she returned, running past me across the lawn. She jumped into her car, backed up—and then she saw mine blocking the drive. She sounded her horn, again and again. A dog barked, and she jumped out and bawled at me. "You bloody fool!" she shouted. "Get that van of yours out of the way!"

The language that came out of her small mouth was like

what you hear in the cattle market on Fridays. I slowly went up and got into my van. I could hear her swearing and the other car tearing off; already it must have turned into the main road. I got into mine, and there we sat, face to face, scowling at each other through our windscreens. I reversed down the long, winding drive, very fast, keeping one eye on her all the time, and turned sharply off the road at the entrance. I don't mind saying that I was showing off. I can reverse a car at speed and put it anywhere to within an inch of where I want to. I saw her face change as she came on, for in her temper she was coming fast down the drive straight at me, radiator to radiator. At the end, she gave one glance of surprise at me, and I think held back a word she had ready as she drove past. At any rate, her mouth was open. Half a dozen cows started from under the trees and went trotting round the field in panic as she went, and the rooks came out of the elms like bits of black paper.

By bad luck, you see, I had arrived in the middle of one of the regular Brackett rows. They were famous in the neighborhood. The Bracketts chased each other round the house, things came out of windows—clothes, boots, anything. Our roundsman said he had once seen a portable radio, playing full on, come flying out, and that it had fallen, still playing, in the roses. Servants came down to the town and said they had had enough of it. Money was usually at the bottom of the trouble. There was a tale going round that when a village girl who worked there got married, Mrs. Brackett gave her a three-shilling alarm clock for a wedding present.

The rows always went the same way. A car would race out of the drive with Noisy in it, and five minutes later Mrs. Brackett would be in her car chasing him, and no one was safe on the roads for twenty miles around. Sometimes it might end quietly in a country pub, with Mrs. Brackett in one bar and Noisy in the other, white-faced and playing hymns on the piano to mock her until she gave in. Other times, it might go on through the night. Noisy, who raced cars, was the better driver, but she was wilder. She would do anything; she once cut through the footpath of the cemetery to catch him on the other side. She sometimes caught him, but more than once her meanness about money would leave her standing. There would be a telephone call to Briggs' garage: Mrs. Brackett had run out of petrol. She was too mean ever to have much more than a gallon in the tank.

"Bless her," Noisy used to say if anyone mentioned these chases to him. "I always rely on the Fairy Queen to run out of gas."

Noisy was a woman hater. His trouble was his habit of saying "Bless you" to the whole female sex.

"Well, I hope you're satisfied," my mother said when I got home. I put Mrs. Brackett's shoe on the table.

"I've made some progress," I said.

My mother looked at the shoe for a long time. Now that I had got something out of Mrs. Brackett, Mother began to think a little less of her. "You'd think a woman with feet like that would dress better," she said.

But what annoyed me was that at some stage in the afternoon's chase Noisy had slipped in and got Mother to cash him a cheque for twenty pounds.

June is the busy time of the year for us. There are all the June weddings. Noisy and Mrs. Brackett must have settled down again somehow, because I saw them driving through

224

the town once or twice. I said to myself: "You wait till the rush is over."

In July, I went up to the Bracketts' house a second time. Rosie, the dark girl who works in our café, came with me, because she wanted to meet her aunt at the main-line station, three or four miles over the hill beyond Heading Mount, and I was taking her on there after I had spoken to Mrs. Brackett. I drove up to the house. The rhododendrons had died, and there were pods on them already going brown. The sun struck warm in front of the house. It was wonderfully quiet.

I left the girl in the car, reading a book, and was working out a sentence to say, when I saw Mrs. Brackett kneeling by a goldfish pond, at the far side of the great lawn. She turned and saw me. I did not know whether to go over the lawn to her or to wait where I was. I decided to go over, and she got up and walked to me. Mother was right about her clothes. This time she was wearing a gaudy tomato-coloured cotton dress that looked like someone else's, and nothing on underneath it. I do not know why it was—whether it was because I was standing on the grass she was walking over, whether it was my anxiety about how to begin the conversation, or whether it was because of her bare white arms, the dawdling manner of her walk, and the inquisitiveness of her eyes—but I thought I was going to faint. When she was two yards away, my heart jumped, my throat closed, and my head was swimming. Although I had often seen her driving through the town, and though I remembered our last meeting all too well, I had never really looked at her before. She stopped, but I had the feeling that she had not stopped but was invisibly walking on until she walked clean through me. My arms went weak. She was amused by the effect she had on me.

"I know who you are," she said. "You are Mr. Fraser's son. Do you want to speak to me?"

I did, but I couldn't. I forgot all the sentences I had prepared. "I've come about our cheque," I said at last. I shouted it. Mrs. Brackett was as startled by my shout as I was. She blushed at the loudness and shock of it—not a light blush but a dark, red, flooding blush on her face and her neck that confused her and made her lower her head like a child caught stealing. She put her hands behind her back like a child. I blushed, too. She walked up and down a yard or two, her head still down, thinking. Then she walked away to the house.

"You'd better come inside," she called back in an offhand way.

You could have put our house into the hall and sitting room of Heading Mount. I had been in that room when I was a boy, helping the waitress when my father was there doing the catering for a party. I do not know what you'd have to pay for the furniture there—thousands, I suppose. She led me through the room to a smaller room beyond it, where there was a desk. I felt I was slowly walking miles. I have never seen such a mess of papers and letters. They were even spread on the carpet. She sat down at the desk.

"Can you see the bill?" she muttered, not looking at me and pointing to the floor.

"I've got it here," I said, taking the bill out of my pocket. She jerked her head. The flush had gone, and now she looked as keen as needles at me.

"Well, sit down," she said.

She took the bill from me and looked at it. Now I could see that her skin was not white but was really pale and clay-coloured, with scores of little cracks in it, and that she was certainly nearer forty than thirty, as Mother always said.

"I've paid this," she said, giving the bill a mannish slap. "I pay every quarter."

"It has been running for three and a half years," I said, more at ease now.

"What?" she said. "Oh, well, I paid something, anyway. This isn't a bill. It's a statement."

"Yes," I said. "We have sent you the bills."

"Where's the date? This hasn't got any date on it."

I got up and pointed to the date.

"It ought to be at the top," she said.

My giddiness had gone. Noisy came into the room. "Hullo, Bob," he said. "I've just been talking to that beautiful thing you have got in the car." He always spoke in an alert, exhausted way about women, like someone at a shoot waiting for the birds to come over. "Have you seen Bob's girl, darling?" he said to her. "I've just offered her the key to my heart." And he lifted the silk scarf he was wearing in the neck of his canary-coloured pullover, and there was a piece of string round his neck with a heavy old door key hanging from it. Noisy gave a twitch to one side of his face.

"Oh, God, that old gag," said Mrs. Brackett.

"Not appreciated, old boy," said Noisy to me.

"Irresistible," said Mrs. Brackett, with an ugly mouth. She turned and spoke to me again, but glanced shrewdly at

Noisy as she did so. "Let me try this one on you," she said. "You've already got my husband's cheque for this bill. I send him down to pay you, and he just cashes them?"

"I'm afraid not, Mrs. Brackett," I said. "That wouldn't be possible."

"You can't get away with that one, my pet," said Noisy. "Are you ready to go out?" He looked at her dress, admiring her figure. "What a target, Bob," he said.

"I don't think we will ask Mr. Fraser's opinion," she said coldly, but very pleased. And she got up and started out of the room, with Noisy behind her.

"You had better send me the bills," she called back to me, turning round from the door.

I felt very, very tired. I left the house and slammed the car door when I got in. "Now she wants the damn bills," I said to Rosie as I drove her up to Tolton station. I did not speak to her the rest of the way. She irritated me, sitting there.

When I got home and told my mother, she was short with me. That was the way to lose customers, she said. I was ruining all the work she and Dad had put into the business. I said if Mrs. Brackett wanted her bills she could come and get them herself. Mother was very shocked.

She let it go for a day or two, but she had to bring it up again. "What are you sulking about?" she said to me one afternoon. "You upset Rosie this morning. Have you done those bills for Mrs. Brackett yet?"

I made excuses, and got in the car and went over to the millers and to the people who make our boxes, to get away from the nagging. Once I was out of the town, in the open

228

country, Mrs. Brackett seemed to be somewhere just ahead of me, round a corner, over a hill, beyond a wood. There she was, trying to make me forget she owed us two hundred and twenty-eight pounds, fourteen and fourpence. The moment she was in my head, the money went out of it. When I got back, late in the evening, Mother was onto me again. Noisy had been in. She said he had been sent down by his wife to ask why I had not brought the bills.

"The poor Wing Commander," my mother said. "Another rumpus up there." (She always gave him his rank if there was a rumour of another quarrel at Heading.) "She never gives him any peace. He's just an errand boy. She does what she likes with him."

"He's been offering you the key to his heart, Mother," I said.

"I don't take any stock of him," Mother said. "Or that pansy 'sweetheart' stuff. Dad was the one and only for me. I don't believe in second marriages. I've no time for jealous women; they're always up to something, like Mrs. Doubleday thinking I spoke to her husband in the bank and she was caught with the chemist, but you always think the Fairy Prince will turn up—it's natural."

It always took a little time getting at what was in Mother's mind, yet it was really simple. She was a good churchwoman, and she thought Noisy was not really married to Mrs. Brackett, because he had been divorced by his first wife. She did not blame Noisy for this—in fact, she admired it, in a romantic way—but she blamed Mrs. Brackett because, by Mother's theories, Mrs. Brackett was still single. And Mother never knew whether to admire single women for holding out or to suspect them of being on the prowl. One thing she was certain of. "Money talks," she said. The thing that made Noisy respectable for her, and as good as being married in church, was that he had married Mrs. Brackett for her money.

She talked like this the night we sat up and did that month's bills, but the next day—and this was the trouble with Mother—it ended in a row. I sent the bills up to Mrs. Brackett by our delivery van.

"That is not the way to behave," Mother said. "You should have taken them yourself."

And before the day was out, Mother was in a temper again. Mrs. Brackett had spoken to her on the telephone and said she had been through the bills and that we had charged her for things she hadn't had, because she'd been in the South of France at the time.

"I told you to go," Mother said to me.

I was angry, too, at being called dishonest. I got out the van and said I was going up at once.

"Oh, that's how it is," said my mother, changing round again. "Her Ladyship snaps her fingers and you go up at once. She's got you running about for her like Noisy. If I ask you to do anything, you don't pay any attention to me. But Mrs. Brackett—she's the Queen of England. Two of you running after her."

Mother was just like that with Father when he was alive. He took no notice. Neither did I. I went up to Heading. A maid let me in, and I sat there waiting in the drawing room. I waited a long time, listening to the bees coming down the chimney, circling lower and lower and then roaring out into the room, like Noisy's car. I could hear Mrs. Brackett talking on the telephone in her study. I could hear now and then what she was saying. She was a great racing woman, and from words she said here and there I would say she was speaking to a bookmaker. One sentence I remember, because I think it had the name of a horse in it, and when I got back home later I looked up the racing news to see if I could find it. "Tray pays on," she said. She came out into the room with the laughter of her telephone call still on her face. I was standing up, with our account book in my hand, and when she saw me the laughter went.

I was not afraid of her any more. "I hear there is some trouble about the bills," I said. "If you've got them, you can check them with the book. I've brought it."

Mrs. Brackett was a woman who watched people's faces. She put on her dutiful, serious, and obedient look, and led me again to the little room where the papers were. She sat down and I stood over her while we compared the bills and the book. I watched the moving of her back as she breathed. I pointed to the items, one by one, and she nodded and ticked the bills with a pencil. We checked for nearly half an hour. The only thing she said was in the middle of it— "You've got a double-jointed thumb: so have I"—but she went right on.

"I can see what it is," I said at the end. "You've mistaken 1953 for '54."

She pushed the book away, and leaned back in the chair against my arm, which was resting on it.

"No, I haven't," she said, her small, unsmiling face looking up into mine. "I just wanted you to come up."

She gazed at me a long time. I thought of all the work

Mother and I had done, and then that Mother was right about Mrs. Brackett. I took my hand from the chair and stepped back.

"I wanted to ask you one or two things," she said, confidingly, "about that property next to the shop. I'll be fair with you. I'm interested in it. Are you? All right, don't answer. I see you are."

My heart jumped. Ever since I could remember, Father and Mother had talked of buying this property. It was their day-dream. They simply liked little bits of property everywhere, and now I wanted it so that we could join the shop and the café.

"I asked because . . ." She hesitated. "I'll be frank with you. The bank manager was talking about it to me today."

My fright died down. I didn't believe that the bank manager—he was Mr. Pickering's brother-in-law—would let my mother down and allow the property to go to Mrs. Brackett without giving us the offer first.

"We want it, of course," I said. And then I suspected this was one of her tricks. "That is why I have been getting our bills in," I said.

"Oh, I didn't think that was it," she said. "I thought you were getting married. My husband says you are engaged to the girl you brought up here. He said he thought you were. Has she any money?"

"Engaged!" I said. "I'm not. Who told him that?"

"Oh," she said, and then a thought must have struck her. I could read it at once. In our town, if you cough in the High Street the chemist up at the Town Hall has got a bottle of cough mixture wrapped up and waiting for you; news travels fast. She must have guessed that when Noisy came down dangling the key to his heart, he could have been round the corner all the time, seeing Rosie.

"I'm glad to hear you're not engaged," Mrs. Brackett said tenderly. "I like a man who works. You work like your father did—God, what an attractive man! You're like him. I'm not flattering you. I saw it when you came up the first time."

She asked me a lot of questions about the shop and who did the baking now. I told her I didn't do it and that I wanted to enlarge the restaurant. "The machine bakeries are getting more and more out into the country," I said. "And you've got to look out."

"I don't see why you shouldn't do catering for schools," she said. "And there's the works" (her father's main factory). "Why don't you get hold of the catering there?"

"You can only do that if you have capital. We're not big enough," I said, laughing.

"How much do you want?" she said. "Two thousand? Three? I don't see why we couldn't do something."

The moment she said "we," I came to my senses. "Here's a funny turn-out," I thought. "She won't pay her bills, but first she's after these shops, and now she's waving two thousand pounds in my face." Everyone in our town knew she was artful. I suppose she thought I was green.

"Not as much as two thousand," I said. "Just the bill," I said, nodding at it.

Mrs. Brackett smiled. "I like you. You're interested in money. Good. I'll settle it." And, taking her chequebook from the top of the desk, she put it in her drawer. "I never pay these accounts by cheque. I pay in cash. I'll get it tomorrow at the bank. I'll tell you what I'll do. You've got a shoe of mine. Bring it up tomorrow evening at, say, half past eight. I'll be back by then and you can have it." She paused, and then, getting up, added quickly: "Half tomorrow, half in October."

It was like dealing with the gypsies that come to your door.

"No, Mrs. Brackett," I said. "I'd like all of it. Now." We stared at each other. It was like that moment months ago when she had driven at me in her car and I had reversed down the drive with one eye watching her and one on the road as I shot back. That was the time, I think, I first noticed her—when she opened her mouth to shout a word at me and then did not shout. I could have stayed like this, looking into her small, pretty, miser's blue eyes, at her determined head, her chopped-off fair hair, for half an hour. It was a struggle.

She was the first to speak, and that was a point gained to me. Her voice shook a little. "I don't keep that amount of money in the house," she said.

I knew that argument. Noisy said she always had two or three hundred pounds in the safe in the wall of her study, and whether this was so or not, I could not help glancing towards it.

"I don't like being dictated to," she said, catching my glance. "I have told you what I will do."

"I think you could manage it, Mrs. Brackett," I said.

I could see she was on the point of flying into one of her tempers, and as far as I was concerned (I don't know why), I hoped she would. Her rows with Noisy were so famous that I must have wanted to see one for myself. And I didn't see why she should get away with it. At the back of my

mind, I thought of all the others down in the town and how
they would look when I said I had got my money out of
Mrs. Brackett.

Yet I wasn't really thinking about the money at all, at
this moment. I was looking at her pretty shoulders.

But Mrs. Brackett did not fly into a temper. She considered me, and then she spoke in a quiet voice that took me
off my guard. "Actually," she said, lowering her eyes, "you
haven't been coming up here after money at all, have you?"

"Well—" I began.

"Sh-h-h!" she said, jumping up from her chair and putting her hand on my mouth. "Why didn't you ring me and
tell me you were coming? I am often alone."

She stepped to the door and bawled out: "Jimmy!" as if
he were a long way off. He was—to my surprise, and even
more to hers—very near.

"Yes, ducky?" Noisy called back from the hall.

"Damn," she said to me. "You must go." And, squeezing
my hand, she went through the drawing room into the hall.

"What time do we get back tomorrow evening?" she
said boldly to Noisy. "Half past eight? Come at half past
eight," she said, turning to me, for I had followed her. "I'll
bring back the cash."

The sight of Noisy was a relief to me, and the sound of
the word "cash" made Noisy brighten.

"Not lovely little bits of money!" he exclaimed.

"Not you," said Mrs. Brackett, glaring at him.

"How did you work it, old boy?" said Noisy later, giving
me one of his most quizzical twitches as he walked with me
to my van. When I drove off, I could see him still standing
there, watching me out of sight.

The Key to My Heart

I drove away very slowly. My mind was in confusion. About half a mile off, I stopped the car and lit a cigarette. All the tales I had heard about Mrs. Brackett came back into my mind. It was one thing to look at her, another thing to know about her. The one person I wished I had with me was Noisy. He seemed like a guarantor of safety, a protection. To have had my thoughts read like that by her filled me with fear.

I finished my cigarette. I decided not to go straight home, and I drove slowly all along the lower sides of the oak woods, so slowly and carelessly that I had to swerve to avoid oncoming cars. I was making, almost without knowing it, for The Green Man, at Mill Cross. There was a girl there I had spoken to once or twice. No one you would know. I went in and asked for a glass of beer. I hardly said a word to her, except about the weather, and then she left the bar to look after a baby in the kitchen at the back. That calmed me. I think the way she gave me my change brought me back to earth and made me feel free of Mrs. Brackett's spell. At any rate, I put the threepence in my pocket and swallowed my beer. I laughed at myself. Mrs. Brackett had gypped me again.

When I got home, it was late, and my mother was morose. She was wearing a black dress she often wore when she was alone, dressed up and ready to go out, yet not intending to, as if now that my father was dead she was free if someone would invite her. Her best handbag was beside her. She was often waiting like this, sitting on the sofa, doing nothing but listening to the clock tick, and perhaps getting up to give a touch to some flowers on the table and then sitting down again. Her first words shook me.

"Mrs. Brackett was down here looking for you," she said sharply. "I thought you were with her. She wants you to be sure to go up tomorrow evening to collect some money when she comes back from Tolton. Where have you been?"

"Let the old bitch post it or bring it in," I said.

Mother was horrified at the idea of Mrs. Brackett soiling her hands with money.

"You'll do as I tell you," she said. "You'll go up and get it. If you don't, Noisy will get his hands on it first. You'd think a woman with all that money would go to a decent hairdresser. It's meanness, I suppose."

And then, of course, I saw I was making a lot of fuss about nothing. Noisy would be there when I went up to Heading. Good old Noisy, I thought; thank God for that. And he'll see I get the money, because she said it in front of him.

So the next evening I went. I put my car near the garage, and the first person I saw was Noisy, standing beside his own car. He had a suitcase in his hand. I went over to him.

"Fairy Queen's been at work," he said. He nodded at his tyres. They were flat. "I'm doing some quick thinking."

At that moment, a top window of the house was opened and someone emptied a suitcase of clothes out of it, and then a shower of cigarettes came down.

"She's tidying," he said. "I've got a quarter of an hour to catch the London train. Be a sweetie-pie and run me over there."

I had arrived once more in the middle of one of the

Brackett rows. Only this time Noisy was leaving it to me. That is how I felt about it. "Hop in," I said.

And when we were off and a mile from Heading, he sat up in the seat and looked round. "Nothing on our tail," he said.

"Have you ever heard of a horse called Tray?" I asked him. "Tray pays something? Tray pays on—that can't be it."

"Tray pays on?" repeated Noisy. "Is it a French horse?"

"I don't know," I said.

"Bloody peasant? Could be," said Noisy. "Sounds a bit frog to me."

We got to Tolton station. Noisy was looking very white and set with hatred. Not until he was standing in the queue getting his ticket did it occur to me what Noisy was doing.

"The first time I've travelled by train for fifteen years," he called to me across from the queue. "Damned serious. You can tell her if you see her"—people stared—"the worm has turned. I'm packing it in for good."

And as he went off to the train, he called: "I suppose you are going back? No business of mine, but I'll give you a tip. If you do, you won't find anything in the kitty, Bob." He gave me his stare and his final twitch. It was like the crack of a shot. Bang on, as he would have said. A bull's-eye.

I walked slowly away as the London train puffed out. I took his advice. I did not go back to Heading.

There were rows and rows between the Bracketts, but there was none like this one. It was the last. The others were a chase. This was not. For only Mrs. Brackett was on the road that night. She was seen, we were told, in all the likely places. She had been a dozen times through the town.

238

Soon after ten o'clock she was hooting outside our house. Mother peeped through the curtains, and I went out. Mrs. Brackett got out of her car and marched at me. "Where have you been?" she shouted. "Where is my husband?"

"I don't know," I said.

"Yes, you do," she said. "You took him to Tolton, they told me."

"I think he's gone to London," I said.

"Don't be a damn liar," she said. "How can he have? His car is up there."

"By train," I said.

"By train," she repeated. Her anger vanished. She looked at me with astonishment. The rich are very peculiar. Mrs. Brackett had forgotten people travel by train. I could see she was considering the startling fact. She was not a woman to waste time staying in one state of mind for long. Noisy used to say of her: "That little clock never stops ticking."

"I see," she said to me sarcastically, nodding out the words. "That's what you and Jimmy have been plotting." She gave a shake to her hair and held her chin up. "You've got your money and you don't care," she said.

"What money is that?" I said.

"What money!" she exclaimed sharply, going over each inch of my face. What she saw surprised her at first. Until then she had been fighting back, but now a sly look came to her; it grew into a smile; the smile got wider and wider, and then her eyes became two curved lines, like crow's wings in the sky, and she went into shouts of laughter. It sounded all down the empty street. She rocked with it.

"Oh, no!" she laughed. "Oh, no, that's too good! That's a winner. He didn't give you a penny! He swiped the lot!"

And she looked up at the sky in admiration of that flying man. She was still grinning at me when she taunted breathlessly: "I mean to say—I mean to say—"

I let her run on.

"It was all or nothing with you, wasn't it?" she said. "And you get nothing, don't you?"

I am not sure what I did. I may have started to laugh it off and I may have made a step towards her. Whatever I did, she went hard and prim, and if ever a woman ended anything, she did then. She went over to the car, got in, and slammed the door.

"You backed the wrong horse when you backed Jimmy," she called out to me.

That was the last of her. No more Mrs. Brackett at the shop. "You won't hear another word from her," my mother said.

"What am I supposed to do—get her husband back?" I said.

By the end of the week, everyone in the town was laughing and winking at me.

"You did the trick, boy," the grocer said.

"You're a good-looking fellow, Bob," the ironmonger said.

"Quite a way with the girls," the butcher said. "Bob's deep."

For when Mrs. Brackett went home that night, she sat down and paid every penny she owed to every shopkeeper in the town. Paid everyone, I say. Bar me.

A NOTE ABOUT THE AUTHOR

V(ICTOR) S(AWDON) PRITCHETT was born in Ipswich, England, on December 16, 1900. He attended Alleyn's School (London). After working in the leather trade and as a commercial traveler and shop assistant in France, he set up as a newspaper correspondent there, in Spain, and in Morocco. Later he became a critic, novelist, and writer of short stories. After World War II he was for two years literary editor of *The New Statesman and Nation*. He has also written for films and radio, and is well known in England as a broadcaster. He has visited both North and South America, and in 1953–4 gave a course of lectures in the Christian Gauss Seminar at Princeton University. He contributes regularly to British and American magazines and to the book review of *The New York Times*. His most recent novel, *Mr. Beluncle*, was published in the United States in 1951, but he is perhaps best known here for *The Spanish Temper* (1954), *The Sailor, Sense of Humour, and Other Stories* (1956), and for three books of criticism: *In My Good Books*, *The Living Novel*, and *Books in General*. Mr. Pritchett is married to a charming Welsh lady, has two children, and lives in London.

June 1961

A NOTE ON THE TYPE

The text of this book was set on the Linotype in JANSON, *a recutting made direct from the type cast from matrices long thought to have been made by Anton Janson, a Dutchman who was a practising type-founder in Leipzig during the years 1668–87. However, it has been conclusively demonstrated that these types are actually the work of Nicholas Kis (1650–1702) a Hungarian who learned his trade most probably from the master Dutch type-founder Dirk Voskens. The type is an excellent example of the influential and sturdy Dutch types that prevailed in England prior to the development by William Caslon of his own incomparable designs, which he evolved from these Dutch faces. The Dutch in their turn had been influenced by Claude Garamond in France. The general tone of Janson, however, is darker than Garamond and has a sturdiness and substance quite different from its predecessors.*

Composed, printed, and bound by Kingsport Press, Inc., Kingsport, Tennessee.
The paper was made by
P. H. Glatfelter Co., Spring Grove, Pennsylvania. Typography and binding
based on designs by

W ARREN 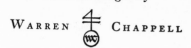 C HAPPELL